Y0-CBI-289

LORD OF PLEASURE

ROGUES TO RICHES #2

ERICA RIDLEY

COPYRIGHT

Copyright © 2017 Erica Ridley
Photograph on cover © VJ Dunraven, PeriodImages
Cover Design © Teresa Spreckelmeyer, Midnight Muse

This is a work of fiction. Names, characters, places, and incidents are the product of the author's imagination or are used fictitiously. Any resemblance to actual events, locales, or persons, living or dead, is purely coincidental.

All rights reserved. Except as permitted under the U.S. Copyright Act of 1976, no part of this publication may be reproduced, distributed, or transmitted in any form or by any means, or stored in a database or retrieval system, without the prior written permission of the author.

ALSO BY ERICA RIDLEY

Rogues to Riches:

Lord of Chance

Lord of Pleasure

Lord of Night

Lord of Temptation

Lord of Secrets

Lord of Vice

Dukes of War:

The Viscount's Tempting Minx

The Earl's Defiant Wallflower

The Captain's Bluestocking Mistress

The Major's Faux Fiancée

The Brigadier's Runaway Bride

The Pirate's Tempting Stowaway

The Duke's Accidental Wife

The 12 Dukes of Christmas:

Once Upon a Duke

Kiss of a Duke

Wish Upon a Duke

Never Say Duke

Dukes, Actually

CHAPTER 1

London, 1817

The comically sketched visage of Michael Rutland, Earl of Wainwright, littered the public-facing windows along the Strand... as well as graced the tea tables and smoking rooms of every fashionable Londoner eager to part with a shilling in exchange for the latest bawdy comic.

Which apparently also included Lord Wainwright's best friends.

So as to ensure the fame of his nocturnal proclivities did not escape the earl's notice, the wretched scoundrels had helpfully strung up a copy of each of his recent caricatures around the salon of his favorite gaming hell.

The Cloven Hoof *used* to be Michael's favorite, anyway.

"Is it true then?" Lord Hawkridge grinned from behind his glass of port. "With naught but a word, the most stalwart of maidens can be smitten by an earl's charms?"

"What words?" Gideon, the owner of the Cloven Hoof, put in before Michael could defend himself. If there was a defense to be had. Gideon held the latest caricature aloft. "No woman alive cares what Wainwright has to *say*. One glimpse of his golden locks and puppy-brown eyes causes them to tumble directly into his arms. Or the closest prone surface."

"I do not have puppy eyes." Michael snatched the print from Gideon's hands.

"Note that he does not deny the other accusations," Hawkridge stage-whispered. "I imagine the caricatures are quite helpful. A rake like Wainwright would likely be unable to recall the names or faces of his many conquests, were they not immortalized for him in the daily comic prints."

Michael ignored both of his friends. All he could see was the dratted sketch. He fought the urge to crumple it in his fist. What would be the point? By now, thousands of copies would be circulating London. He tried to be objective.

Today's drawing was both better and worse than the others. When he'd attended the previous night's soirées, he had purposefully abstained from his habitual flirtatiousness, with the intent of proving his name need not be synonymous with "debauched rake."

After all, Michael's only lovers were women who were no strangers to the art of seduction. He had no interest in despoiling virgins. He attended society events because he liked good company, great food, and fine entertainment.

There was no need for messy entanglements. Michael enjoyed dancing whether it led to a secluded balcony or whether it was simply a waltz with a pretty stranger he'd never see again in his life. He simply enjoyed women's company. He'd hoped last night's careful, above reproach comportment would prove once and for all that he wasn't on the prowl, for God's sake.

Well… it had worked, and hadn't.

The italicized title below the caricature read "*Lord of Pleasure.*" An eminently recognizable sketch of himself at the previous day's biggest crush took center stage, surrounded by dozens of overcome damsels dropping into a swoon, when all his overly gallant form had managed to say was, "Good aftern—"

"Ha, ha, ha," Michael said sourly as he flung the drawing back to Gideon.

No wonder the gaming hell owner had said no one was interested in anything Michael had to say. Based on that evidence, the marriage-minded debutantes were eager to become his countess, and the pleasure-minded widows and courtesans merely wished to experience for themselves the rumors of his sensual prowess.

Not that there was anything wrong with pleasure! That was why it was *called* "pleasure." Because it was pleasurable to all parties involved. Who cared how two consenting adults spent an evening in each other's company? Half of London had mistresses. All the other affairs in caricaturists' drawings were scandalous because they were famous cuckolds. He was the only hapless gentleman to stay in the scandal columns based on reputation alone.

"It's rubbish," he said as he took a seat at the bar. "Do the caricaturists have no real scandals to draw?"

Gideon uncorked a fresh bottle of wine. "That *is* the humor. Others have to perform foolish or wicked acts to get half the attention that you attract just by walking into a room."

"When an unwed earl with a sizable purse walks into a room," corrected a barmaid as she poured the wine.

Another barmaid let her gaze travel Michael's form with a suggestive grin. "I don't think it's just the size of his earldom that attracts the ladies."

He clenched his jaw in frustration. Even the serving wenches were too blinded by the *Lord of Pleasure* image to see beyond it. Then again, title-hunters were even worse.

"I have no interest in a woman who cares more about becoming a countess than she does about the man she'd wed to do so. Those women would marry a toad if it meant gaining a title."

"We should all be so fortunate," Hawkridge muttered.

Michael winced. The penniless marquess was now on the hunt for an heiress with enough blunt to save the marquessate, but thus far had found no luck. "Your case is different," he said quickly. "I hope you find an heiress with a heart as big as her pocketbook. You deserve a happy marriage."

"Now you're giving relationship advice?" Gideon didn't bother to hide his burst of laughter. "Have you ever had the same mistress for more than a week before you tired of her?"

"Intercourse is not a *relationship*," Michael corrected haughtily. He glanced away before Gideon realized he was more right than he knew.

In the nine-and-twenty years of his life, Michael had spent the latter half of it in pursuit of pleasure... and had particularly enjoyed this past decade. The one thing he had not yet experienced was an actual relationship. He'd been too focused on flirtation to ever come close to falling in love. If the sketches lining the Cloven Hoof were any indication, he had become too good at his task. Ladies couldn't see past his Lord of Pleasure reputation. And to the men, Michael was simply... a caricature.

"I'll change my image," he said suddenly.

Hawkridge choked on his wine. "You'll what?"

"Reshape my image," Michael repeated. After all, he had countless other interests. Nature, music, astronomy. The caricaturists didn't know about those pastimes because they were solitary endeavors. Surely it couldn't be *that* hard to prove he was more than a pretty face. "I very much hope my future wife finds endless pleasure in our marriage bed, but that is not the only thing I have to offer."

5

The entire gaming hell went silent at this pronouncement.

Even Gideon stared back at him in amusement. "What else do you have to offer?"

"Honestly, Wainwright." Lord Hawkridge gestured at this morning's caricature. "Just being present when you enter a room is enough to get a lady's name mentioned in the scandal columns. You couldn't stay out of them if you tried."

"I could." Michael rolled back his shoulders. Perhaps it would not be easy, but it was far from impossible. "In fact, I will. I'll prove to you and to London at large that there's more to the Earl of Wainwright than mere scandal fodder."

"How will you prove that?" Hawkridge asked doubtfully. "By performing some grand public feat? Or simply staying out of the scandal columns?"

Gideon's betting book thumped onto the bar. "Let's limit it to staying out of the scandal columns, just to give the poor sap a chance. How long do you think he can go without his name in the gossip columns or his face in the comics? A week? A fortnight?"

"That's a fool's bet," Hawkridge protested. "Did you not see today's drawing? Wainwright wouldn't be able to stay out of the papers for a single day, much less reshape his *image*."

"Thirty days," Michael said. Hadn't he wanted to cut the pages on the new nature journals he'd bought for his library? The time would fly by. "If I stay out of the scandal columns for an entire month, will you agree that I've changed my image?"

"You'd have changed your entire personality." The marquess shook his head. "You *are* the Lord of Pleasure. It cannot be done."

"Not his personality," Gideon said slowly. He pushed the *Lord of Pleasure* caricature back toward Hawkridge. "Take another look. Wainwright is right. They're not drawing anything he *did*. They draw society's perception of him. I'll give you forty days."

"Forty it is." Michael inclined his head. It was just a matter of perspective. Had the caricaturists drawn him admiring the sky with his telescope or reading nature journals, there would be no story.

"Twenty quid!" called a voice from one of the gaming tables. "I've got twenty quid that says the earl won't make a fortnight without being in the papers."

"I've got fifty that says he shan't make it to the end of the week," called another.

"I've got no money at all," Hawkridge muttered, "but only a fool would let this wager pass him by. Put me down for ten quid, Gideon. I'll scrape up the blunt somewhere."

Michael stared at him. "You're a true friend."

"I'm adding a hundred-pound rider," Gideon announced to the room. "If he does make the forty days, it'll be because he found a wife. Any takers?"

The room was silent.

Even Michael stared at Gideon in disbelief. "I

promised to stay out of the papers, not to become a monk. I've no intention of getting leg-shackled."

He would find a countess and beget an heir, but not for another ten years, at least. A proper lady would want a bland, boring life. Until then, he would not allow life's pleasures to pass him by.

"Now that you're going to be respectable for a month, what are you going to do with your time?" called one of the gamblers. "Go to sewing circles and the Grenville musicales?"

"Ha," called another. "The only music Wainwright likes is the music he makes with his 'models' in the harp room."

"What if I do? Anything that happens inside private chambers is fair game, as long as it stays out of the scandal columns," Michael reminded them as he slid one hundred pounds across the bar to take Gideon's wager.

Forty days of publicly respectable behavior. No caricatures. No gossip. No wife.

How hard could it be?

CHAPTER 2

*M*iss Camellia Grenville stood just outside her mother's sitting room, too nervous to bring herself to knock upon the door. She inspected her skirt for wrinkles.

Why had she been summoned to her mother's private parlor? Camellia was never summoned anywhere. She was the *good* daughter. Her headstrong younger sisters were frequently called to the carpet, but Camellia? Never. She was the sensible one. The shy one. The elder spinster sister who would be perfectly happy to live the rest of her quiet life in the same living quarters she'd enjoyed since leaving the nursery years earlier.

Camellia never rocked the boat because she liked her life exactly as it was. Comfortable. Predictable. Never more than an arm's reach from home and family. Surrounded with books and music and laughter. Her biggest fear was that one day, her parents would tire of the unseemly rambunctiousness of their youngest two girls, and

9

marry Bryony and Dahlia off to the first available suitors, leaving the house preternaturally quiet and Camellia all alone.

Her hands went clammy. Perhaps that was exactly what was happening. And she, as elder sister, would be expected to break the news.

She swallowed hard and forced herself to knock upon the door.

"Daughter, is that you? Come inside, darling. Tea will arrive at any moment."

Camellia warmed. Not only had she never before received an unexpected summons, she also had never been invited to a private tea. The idea sounded lovely. Tea with Mother would no doubt be quite a departure from Camellia's usual spot nestled into a safe corner of the girls' sitting room to watch the younger two giggle and argue. Yet the lump of worry in her stomach only increased.

She smoothed the wrinkles from her day dress and entered the room.

Mother sat perched on the edge of a chaise longue, her silver-streaked brown locks expertly pinned into a gorgeous chignon. With a wave of her perfectly manicured fingers, she gestured for Camellia to take the seat opposite.

"Sit, darling. A lady must never stand about like a servant awaiting orders."

Camellia sat, well aware that doing so was still following orders.

"Is something amiss, Mother?"

"Amiss?" Mother clasped her fingers to her

chest in something akin to rapture. "Quite the opposite. The future is finally falling into place. Darling, you're going to be *married*!"

"I'm..." Words failed her as Camellia gripped the edges of a wingback chair, grateful than she'd taken the advice to sit down before her mother's pronouncement could knock her over. "Me? Married? To *whom*?"

"His name is Mr. Irving Bost, and he is a mature, respectable gentleman in want of a mature, respectable bride. He has chosen you for that honor. Congratulations, darling."

Camellia stared at her mother in utter stupefaction. Not because she didn't understand what was happening—but because she *did*. The news could not have been worse.

In polite conversation, a "mature" gentleman meant he was old enough to be her father. Conversely, a "mature" bride meant that Camellia was a spinster, and ought to consider herself lucky to have him.

She had a vague recollection of meeting Mr. Bost. He wasn't especially handsome, but he had all his hair and his teeth and a large library and a kind smile. He was unexceptional and unobjectionable.

And if she didn't stop this right now, he was going to be her husband.

"He's twice my age," she stammered in desperation.

Her mother airily waved a hand. "Many marriages are that way. Why, I was twenty years younger than your father, and everything worked out fine, did it not? If anything, Mr. Bost's age is an advantage. He has already sown his wild oats and is ready to settle down. Why would you want an immature lad when you could have a grown man?"

"Not immature," Camellia interjected, unable to hide her frustration. "I simply meant less…"

Less what? *Stodgy* had been the first word to come to mind, followed by *boring*, both complaints that would have impressed her mother as being quite ironic indeed.

Unfortunately, Miss Camellia Grenville was not known for being stodgy and boring. Miss Camellia Grenville wasn't known at all, because she *was* stodgy and boring.

In fact, she found it unlikely that Mr. Bost— or, well, anyone—would have called upon her parents seeking the nondescript elder sister's hand in marriage. More likely, he had glimpsed Bryony or Dahlia somewhere outrageous and had come in search of one of them, only to be told that the Grenvilles could not possibly part with one of their younger daughters until the eldest had made her match, and wouldn't Camellia do just as well?

"Is it my dowry?" she asked weakly.

The daughter of a baron was not the same as the daughter of a duke or an earl, but her family was by no means poor. All three sisters boasted a respectable dowry, expressly designed for the purpose of attracting suitors.

Mother laughed. "Darling, you needn't worry about money ever again. Mr. Bost may not be Croesus, but his accounts are quite flush. You shan't want for a single thing."

Wouldn't she? Camellia pushed the thought away and forced herself to smile. She would make the best of the situation. She always did.

"We would live here in London?" she asked.

"Northumberland, actually," Mother replied. "Mr. Bost has a picturesque estate not far from the Scottish border. Positively enchanting, he tells us."

All the way north to Scotland? Horror engulfed Camellia. Nowhere could be farther from London, from her family, from everything and everyone she knew and loved. That wasn't enchantment. That was hell.

She tried to think. What else did she recall about Mr. Bost? He admired the out-of-doors, but only from afar. His propensity to wheeze during any exertion meant he not only wouldn't be riding horses with her across the rolling hills, but also Camellia's dreams of nature walks and other such activities with her future husband would stay just that. Dreams.

Mr. Bost wasn't destitute. He did not need her dowry. He wanted a nice quiet mouse to live in his nice quiet cottage in the middle of the nice quiet countryside. Who better than Camellia Grenville? Her fingers went numb. This was a disaster. She might be the answer to his problems, but he would be the cause of hers.

She didn't *want* to seal herself inside nature-proof walls with no one but him for company. They had never spent more than a few moments together. He was a stranger. Her sisters were her best friends. His home was at least a six-day drive. Even if he were a royal prince, living so far from her family would be a nightmare. Her hands trembled at the thought.

"Look, darling." Mother lifted a hand toward the door as a pair of maids brought in the tea service. "I had Cook send up your favorite lemon cakes. Have as many as you like. We're celebrating!"

Camellia was closer to screaming than celebrating.

She simply could not possibly bring herself to do it. Could not, would not, wed a man twice her age and live the rest of her life far away from her family.

Except her parents weren't giving her any other options.

If Mr. Bost wished to have her, then so he would. That was what being a dutiful daughter meant. This was her path. Camellia had always been the good girl. She would do as she was told. As she had always done.

And because she would do the right thing—because she was already firmly on the shelf and her desperate parents had despaired of receiving any offers for her at all—by accepting this suitor, Camellia's younger sisters could finally have the attention they'd been denied due to the presence of an unwed elder sister in the house. She should be pleased. Relieved to be out of their hair.

Mr. Bost was not her choice. She couldn't be more miserable.

Her stomach sank. She'd always dreamed that choosing a suitor would be the one moment in her life when she was actually able to do what *she* wanted. But it was not to be. Once she was married, it wouldn't even be her well-meaning parents making all her decisions for her. It would be her husband. A stranger whom she would be expected to obey in all things. Even if it meant her own skin had become a cage.

"Such a fine match," Mother said with obvious pride. "Mr. Bost is a kind man. He might even allow you to sing a little when you're not occupied with your other responsibilities. Even if he is not so musically inclined, I am certain no husband could object to you humming quietly in a separate room."

The thought failed to conjure images of wedded bliss. Camellia's fingers shook. Singing was the one thing she loved almost as much as her family. It was more than a mere hobby. It was her passion. The only time she truly felt free. And now perhaps that too would be gone forever. "He's still downstairs speaking with Father, I presume?"

"Oh, I'm afraid not. Mr. Bost left at once. He must be out of London by now."

"He... left?" Camellia echoed in disbelief.

Mother selected another teacake. "It's a very

long drive back to Northumberland, darling. He was wise not to dawdle. There are highwaymen in the dark."

"But... did he not wish to talk to *me*?"

Mother's forehead creased in genuine befuddlement. "About what?"

About what, indeed. Camellia rubbed her temples in frustration. This was a nightmare. She had never felt more like a nonentity. And yet, what had she expected?

Her parents had never asked for her opinion about anything at all. Not because they were cruel, but because it had not occurred to them that she might have one. They never asked what their daughter thought or wanted because it was irrelevant. She knew what was expected of her. They were confident she would do the right thing. As she always did.

"I'm delighted for you, darling." Mother leaned forward to give Camellia an excited pat on the knee. "It couldn't have happened to a more deserving young lady. You've never given your father or me the least bit of trouble, and we know you'll do the same for Mr. Bost. Your father even told him so. 'A perfect wife.' Mr. Bost will return in a month to sign the contract and submit the first banns. You'll be wed in no time!"

Camellia was far from delighted. Her flesh crawled at the thought of being married to a man who chose a wife without consulting the woman in question.

Yes, she knew such circumstances were not

unusual. There were many young ladies desperate to secure their futures, who would consider Mr. Bost a fine catch. Amongst Camellia's set, marriages were often business transactions, political deals, necessary evils to beget an heir. But a part of her had always hoped…

Her teacup rattled against its saucer, and she placed it back on the tray before it fell from her lap. Her appetite had long since vanished.

"Might I be excused, Mother? The news is… something of a shock."

"Oh, certainly, darling. You must be dying to share your good fortune with your sisters. Perhaps they will even come to visit you someday!"

Her smile brittle, Camellia pushed herself out of the chair and down the hall before her mother's well-wishes could destroy her mood even further. Panic sluiced through her veins.

A fine pickle she'd got herself into this time. Northumberland. Mr. Bost. Impossible. There had to be a way out.

Her place was here, with her family. Her sisters counted on her for companionship and advice. She couldn't leave them. Because of her practical nature and logical mind, her sisters had always considered Camellia the "smart" one. What would they think now? She certainly didn't feel clever. She felt trapped. Soon, she would be expected to trade the life of a wallflower for one of even more isolated domesticity. Her skin went cold.

If she were a wallflower by choice, by nature,

perhaps the prospect would not seem so grim. But she had always done what was expected of her not because of a personal affinity for propriety, but because *someone* had to be respectable. Their brother Heath was clearly unsuited for the task, and besides—men were judged by a completely different standard.

Which left Camellia. Elder sister to two incorrigible dreamers. Bryony, the hoyden, and Dahlia, the big heart. Both had always looked up to Camellia. Been scolded by their parents that they should be more like their sister. But this was not a path Camellia wished them to follow. She hoped they might find love matches.

Or at least be granted a token consultation prior to presenting themselves to their father.

With a sigh, she peered into the sisters' shared sitting room. As usual, the girls were in the midst of a heated, animated discussion.

"Lord Wainwright is the soap scum from the bottom of a communal bathing bucket," Dahlia declared from her habitual perch in one of the large bay windows. She was far too restless to sit behind an escritoire, and preferred to employ a travel writing desk on her knees so she could look out upon London. Today, her red-rimmed eyes were not on the city, but on the battered correspondence piled on her lap. "He has ruined my life, and the lives of two dozen innocent young ladies in the process."

Camellia's heart caught in dismay. She had thought her day was as bad as it could get, but that was before someone had hurt her sister. She clenched her fists as anger flooded through her.

Bryony set down her curling tongs to meet her sister's gaze in the looking glass. "The earl is unquestionably a shallow, arrogant Corinthian, but I am not certain you can refer to the residents of a school for wayward girls as 'innocents.'" She frowned in consideration. "Or ladies."

"That's the *point* of the school." Dahlia rubbed her face, her eyes dejected. "To teach proper comportment and give them a chance for a better future. Or at least that had been the plan, until Lord Wainwright convinced everyone to retract their donations."

Camellia's mouth fell open in horror. Good heavens. Of all the despicable—

"He *what?*" Bryony leapt up from the dressing table. "The school lost all its donations? That *is* unconscionable. I thought you were exaggerating about Lord Wainwright ruining innocent lives, but without that money... What are you going to do?"

"I don't know," Dahlia said bleakly. "Without donations, I cannot continue to purchase food or pay the chef or the instructors." Spine curved dejectedly, she leaned against the window pane. "We can't toss the girls back out to the streets. But if they stay... they starve." She lifted her head. "I suppose I could always go back to—"

"You will *not* return to thievery." Camellia marched into the room, her tone final. The threat was real.

When Dahlia was much younger, she had once been caught stealing food and garment scraps earmarked for the rubbish bin and delivering them to rookery orphanages instead. Their parents had very nearly disowned her. They asserted that neither sculleries nor rookeries were the place for a lady.

"It's not thievery when it's *trash*," Dahlia insisted. "If the rich have no use for their rubbish, why not give it to someone who does?"

"Fair point." Bryony nodded slowly. "We cannot let her wards starve or sell themselves in the streets. Lord Wainwright has ruined the only chance to raise reputable money. What else is she supposed to do?"

"Nothing." Camellia tightened her fingers in determination. "I will handle it."

"How?" Dahlia's shoulders slumped. "There is no other way to raise money. My funds will be dry within the next month."

Camellia took a deep breath. She *would* handle it. She had been saving her sisters for years. This might well be her last chance to do so. She squared her shoulders. "I shall ask my husband for the money."

"Your *what?*" A pile of wrinkled correspondence fell from Dahlia's lap as she shoved her writing desk aside. "What husband?"

"It is my honor to inform you…" Camellia struggled to keep the hitch from her voice. "It seems Father has betrothed me to a mature, respectable stranger in want of a mature, respectable wife. In six weeks' time, I will be Mrs. Bost."

"What?" Dahlia repeated in a horrified whisper. "Cam, *no.*"

"Mother assures me his accounts are quite flush. Since he has no particular need for my dowry, certainly he can spare a portion for a worthy cause."

"You cannot mean to marry him." Bryony's countenance was pale.

"What choice do we have? The marriage contract is being drawn up now. If at least one good thing can come of it…" Camellia swallowed. "Even if he has no wish to become a permanent patron, with luck his donation will carry the school forward until Dahlia can attract new funding."

"*Damn* that Lord Wainwright." Bryony's eyes flashed. "This is all his fault. Why couldn't he have left us alone?"

"Watch your tongue," Dahlia said tonelessly. Her shoulders curved. "Ladies shouldn't curse. Or steal rubbish. Or betroth themselves to save someone else."

Camellia eased down onto the fainting couch and hoped she wouldn't need it. "Tell me what happened. Why would Lord Wainwright wish to dismantle a deportment school? What exactly did he do?"

"He doesn't know the first thing about my school." Dahlia's lips flattened. "The brute managed to jeopardize the entire enterprise simply by

21

being the sort of person he is: a rich, handsome, frivolous rake."

Camellia reared back, aghast. "He didn't even realize what he'd done?"

"Do rakehells ever?" Dahlia rubbed her temples. "I was at Lady Kingsley's dinner party. I would still be there now, but I couldn't bring myself to stay after..." Her gaze unfocused. "The ladies at the table have supported many charitable causes over the years, and had agreed to help fund mine. We were just finalizing the details when Lord Wainwright strode into our midst."

Bryony twisted her lips. "All it takes is a single glance from his entrancing hazel eyes and every woman in the room starts fluttering her fan to her bosom to calm her racing heart. You know what he's like. So handsome it's hard to breathe."

Like her sisters and the rest of the ton, Camellia had once been just such a ninny. Every debutante dreamed of dancing with the rakish earl. The spinsters and the widows dreamed of far more. Caricaturists from Gillray to Cruikshank delighted in chronicling the swath Lord Wainwright cut through the seas of heaving bosoms. Now that the war with Napoleon was over and Beau Brummel had fled to France, the scandal columns had little else to report than the foibles of the ton.

Camellia wished so many of the caricatures didn't also happen to be true.

"Let me guess," she said with a sigh. "One heated gaze from his angelic visage and those featherbrains forgot they were in the midst of a conversation that had nothing to do with a man."

"Worse." Dahlia sighed. "He told them he was dazzled by all their beauty and accomplishments already, and asked why they would want to create more competition for themselves."

Camellia gasped. "Destitute girls aren't *competition*. They're *children*."

"My students will never attend a ton soirée no matter how high the marks they score in deportment," Dahlia agreed. "Lord Wainwright might have been teasing, but the effect was the same. Lady Upchurch was the first to withdraw her donation and declare herself far too clever to do such a foolish thing. After that, the others had no choice but to follow suit."

"What did Lord Wainwright say when he realized he'd placed the entire school in financial peril?"

"He didn't. He left the moment he set hearts a-flutter. We were not the only females in the room, and a rake does have to make his rounds." Dahlia lifted her chin, her eyes hard. "Someone really ought to take that man down a peg or two."

A part of Camellia couldn't help but agree. She did not condone vindictive behavior, but at the very least a man with that much power over his peers should be made to understand how deeply his thoughtlessness could affect others. Instead, his shamelessly rakehell ways were fêted by the gentlemen and cooed after by the ladies. She curled her lip. He was exactly the sort of self-centered, arrogant scoundrel that she despised the most.

"I agree." Bryony retrieved her forgotten curling tongs and frowned at her reflection. "I hope I get to be the one. Wainwright deserves it." She made a sappy expression over her shoulder. "Although... When we're done taking him down a peg, a girl might consider unbuttoning that chiseled chest a button or two while she's at it."

Dahlia's eyes flashed. "If you so much as smile at that insufferable rake, I shall never speak to you again."

"Never fear," Bryony assured her quickly. "I would never flirt with any bounder who hurt my sister. Instead, I shall console myself with admiring the occasional manly form from afar. Or perhaps many manly forms." She gave a suggestive wink. "Tonight I am attending one of Lambley's masquerades."

Camellia gasped in shock... and envy. A secret part of her often wished she could be as confident and carefree as her youngest sister. "You cannot mean one of the Duke of Lambley's scandalous masquerades. Those gatherings are synonymous with hedonistic abandon. If anyone finds out you attended, your reputation—"

"It's a masquerade," Bryony pointed out. "No one recognizes anyone. That's the whole point... and a perfect distraction. I have been waiting to hear back from my solicitor for so long, I shall go mad without a diversion."

Camellia opened her mouth to respond, then

changed her mind. They could all do with a diversion. Whoever Bryony's solicitor was, he
would be unlikely to come up with a fast solution
for the financial situation at Dahlia's school. But
as long as Camellia managed to talk her soon-to-
be fiancé into donating as soon as they were married, perhaps it would buy enough time for a
more permanent solution to be found.

"The masquerade is tonight?" she asked instead. There was no point asking how Bryony
had wrangled one of the limited, coveted invitations. Camellia's youngest sister was a force of
nature.

"Ten to dawn." Bryony glanced at the clock on
the mantel and grimaced. "Which gives me only a
few hours to curl my uncurlable hair, dress in my
most shocking gown—specially commissioned
just for this occasion—and finally discover precisely what goes on at those infamous parties."

A knock sounded upon the door.

Dahlia sprang up from the window seat and
raced to answer. "Perhaps someone has changed
her mind about the donations."

A footman stood in the corridor with a folded
missive upon a platter. "A letter has arrived for
Miss Bryony."

Dahlia trudged back across the room and
slumped against the window without another
word.

"It's my solicitor!" Bryony's face lit up, then
immediately fell. "There's a small window of opportunity for us to speak, but only if we meet at

once." She groaned. "It seems I am not going to a masquerade. I'm going to a barrister's office." She glanced up at her sisters. "One of you needs to use my invitation. It was too hard to come by to let the opportunity go to waste. And then of course you *must* describe everything you see. I shall be suffering in abject envy."

For a fleeting moment, Camellia wished she were both foolish enough and fearless enough to say yes. She forced herself to remain silent. Sometimes it was difficult to shake off such bouts of wistfulness, but she would be a married woman soon and ought to act like one. No matter how little pleasure the notion brought.

Dahlia shook her head. "The last thing I'm in a humor for is a party. I intend to stay hunched over a desk, scouring each page of *Debrett's Peerage* until I scrounge up a few new names to cover the ones Lord Wainwright turned away."

"Then Cam wins." Bryony thrust the invitation away from her face as if its proximity caused physical pain. "Take it before I decide to cancel the solicitor. A masquerade can be life changing."

"I can't." Camellia backed away from her sister's outstretched hand. "You could go another time."

"There won't be another time." Bryony's voice was urgent. "Repeat invitations are only given to guests who accept the previous invitation. You have no idea how scarce this opportunity is. You *have* to go."

"I cannot," Camellia repeated, trying not to stammer. "What if someone recognized me?"

"They will not be able to. You'll wear a mask the entire night, like everyone else." Bryony pushed the invitation into Camellia's hand. "In the extremely unlikely event that some bloodhound catches a Grenville scent, just claim you're me. It'll be too dark to discern eye color, and we've all got the same dark hair."

"No one would believe it was you anyway," Dahlia added from the window seat. "The only public routs you attend are when Mother forces you to sing at the family soirée musicale."

"Nobody *forces* her," Bryony objected hotly. "Cam likes to sing. Everyone likes it when she sings. From the moment she opens her mouth, no one even notices my violin. She's more talented than anyone we've ever seen at Drury Lane, you must admit."

"The point is, *Cam* wouldn't know that because she never leaves this house. She's as cloistered as a nun. Which means you're right—no one would ever guess it was her." Dahlia leaned forward as some of the sparkle returned to her eyes. "Say yes, Cam. You'll be like a spinster spy. I cannot wait to hear your shocked, conservative observations."

The warmth Camellia felt at their compliments vanished at "spinster spy." Six-and-twenty was older than the average debutante, but still a far cry from some stooping, elderly aunt. She bit back a terse reply about which of them ought to be cloistered. Her sisters were only one and two years younger than her, but sometimes it felt like a lifetime.

A lifetime of wasted opportunities, she realized belatedly. Of comporting herself as a lady was meant to behave, or a daughter, or an elder sister, or a spinster, or anything at all except however Camellia herself might wish. Soon she would be trading all that in for the role of wife. Another prescribed set of rules and regulations to govern her every word and thought.

Being someone else for a few hours first was tempting, indeed.

"It's an absurd idea," she said instead. "No one would ever believe it."

"Of course it's an absurd idea," Dahlia agreed. "That does not mean you shouldn't do it. There won't be a second chance. Unless you think Mr. Bost is likely to take you to scandalous masquerades?"

Mature, respectable Mr. Bost wasn't likely to take her anywhere but Northumberland. A world away from her sisters… and adventure.

Camellia hesitated. As a girl, she had never once done anything rebellious. And she wasn't betrothed yet. Not for a few more weeks.

Yet, much as she would like to have a mad night of freedom, she could not make herself agree to the scheme. It was reckless. Irresponsible. Wild. Everything Camellia had never been and suddenly longed to be, more than anything.

"I wish I could," she said softly. "I'm afraid I

shall have to be brave and prepare for my future position as Mrs. Bost. It will be far easier to accept my destiny than to tempt fate with risky behavior."

"Bravery isn't what you do when it's easy," Bryony said in surprise. "Bravery is what you do when it's hard."

Camellia sent her a dubious look.

"I tend to think all Bryony's ideas are terrible," Dahlia put in slowly. "But if you would truly go… then I think you ought. Shouldn't we accept destiny only once we know what the choices are?"

Camellia hugged herself. "A masquerade cannot change one's destiny. Destiny *means* no choice."

"Then why not go?" Bryony held up a stunning ball gown with puffed sleeves, a plunging neckline, and yards of sumptuous sky blue silk. "I daresay this will attract more intriguing options than any dance card at Almack's."

Dahlia let out a slow whistle as Bryony turned about with the dress. "All of the options deliciously wicked, one supposes."

Bryony winked. "Only if Cam's lucky."

"I don't feel lucky," she admitted. Yet her skin tingled as if the night were already touched with magic. "I feel as if I only have a month to live."

Bryony grinned. "Then make the most of it."

"I'm going to regret this," Camellia muttered as she succumbed to temptation. She flung her arms wide in dramatic fashion. "Dress me like I'm

4

a princess in a fairy story. Tonight, I will pretend to be someone else."

Dahlia squealed as loud as Bryony and leapt from the window seat to help with the transformation.

In their younger days, all three sisters had spent countless hours dressing each other in old, elegant outfits their mother no longer wore, and dressing each other's hair in minute, elaborate styles.

Although they had since grown into young women with designated ladies' maids to mind their appearances, they could not risk one of the servants discovering their plans. Camellia would have to trust that her sisters would do it right.

She let them outfit her as befit the occasion, from the satin ribbons holding up her silk stockings to the rakish ostrich feather curving over a pile of ringlets they'd curled in her hair.

When at last they declared her properly attired for a masquerade, the woman staring back at Camellia in the looking glass no longer resembled the inconspicuous, forgettable wallflower she had been for the previous six-and-twenty years.

The masked lady with the rouged full lips and voluptuous sapphire blue gown would catch the attention of any gentleman in possession of a heartbeat. Camellia's pulse raced at the shocking difference.

"I don't look like a story princess," she gasped,

light-headed. "I look like a seductress of loose morals."

"Perfect!" Bryony exclaimed in delight. "You're going to a licentious masquerade full of rakish gentlemen and night birds of loose morals. You want to blend in."

"Dance scandalously close with anyone you fancy," Dahlia added with a wink. "Just mind not to lose your mask."

CHAPTER 3

*C*amellia alighted from the hackney cab with a flutter of nervous excitement. The hired hack had been stuck in the queue of carriages inching toward the Lambley ducal residence for almost an hour. The mere act of arriving had taken so long that her initial trepidation had been replaced by impatience.

Before tonight, she had been so focused on staying inconspicuous that she'd failed to live her life while she'd still had the freedom to do so. Now that she had committed to stealing a few hours of anonymity, it was all she could do not to race up the duke's front steps and immerse herself in the crowd of masked revelers.

But first, she had to get past the gatekeeper at the door.

In order to verify each guest's invitation, only one set of passengers at a time was allowed to disembark each carriage. Camellia was all alone as she strode toward the entrance with what she

hoped was the relaxed, confident stride of a frequent party guest and not the half-terrified nervous mince of a shy wallflower impersonating
her vivacious younger sister.

The door swung open as she reached the final
step.

A chestnut-haired man with a black mask and
a friendly smile welcomed her inside a marble
vestibule with a small fire and a large crystal
chandelier.

He closed the door, then held out a white-
gloved hand. "Invitation, please."

Camellia's fingers shook as she retrieved the
embossed parchment from her reticule and
placed it into his hand.

The doorkeeper glanced down at the invitation, then up at her. He said nothing. He simply
waited.

Was there a secret passphrase? Sweat prickled
at the nape of Camellia's neck. Bryony hadn't
mentioned a secret passphrase. If Camellia were
turned away at the door in front of an endless
line of carriages... She gulped. It wouldn't matter
that no one could recognize her. Camellia would
kill her sister anyway.

"My apologies," the man said, his voice flat.
"You are not Bryony Grenville."

"I... Of course I am," Camellia stammered.
"Who else would I be?"

The doorkeeper gazed back at her
impassively.

No. She had not come this far to quit this

soon. She rolled back her shoulders with renewed determination. "I am absolutely Miss Grenville."

The man tilted his head to consider her anew.

She tried not to melt into a puddle of nervous embarrassment at his scrutiny. It wasn't working. She was about to be tossed out on her ear.

"You are not Bryony," he said slowly, "but you might well be a Miss Grenville. Take off your mask."

"I... What? No! This—this is a masquerade," she blurted. "Anonymity is the reason everyone is here."

The doorkeeper crossed his arms. "If I don't know who you are, you aren't allowed inside. Either you take off your mask, or you return home. Your choice."

She hesitated, then untied her mask.

His glance upon her naked visage scarcely lasted a moment before he motioned for her to retie the mask. "Very well."

She blinked. "Very well... what?"

He tossed her invitation into the fire, then crossed over to an open journal atop a waist-high, fluted column and scribbled something on one of its pages in black ink. "Welcome to the masquerade, Miss Grenville."

She sent him a doubtful glance. "Did you just write my name in that book?"

"I enter a coded cipher known only to Lambley and myself. Guest privacy is the sole concern the duke prizes as much as their safety."

"But how..." She swallowed. "How did you know I wasn't Bryony?"

"I take special care with verifying all first-time invitation recipients. After taking your name, I allowed the silence to stretch on for some time." His smile was kind. "You withstood the awkwardness admirably. Your sister, however, is not exactly known for her patience in suffering delays or silence."

Camellia's cheeks heated at the doorkeeper's frankness. If anything, his assessment of their character was an understatement. Bryony would have sashayed into the vestibule, teased the doorkeeper with a flirtatious remark, and all but strutted into the hidden chambers without a second thought. Camellia gulped. She should never have taken her sister's place. "Might others recognize me?"

He shook his head. "I had the advantage of having my expectations set by seeing your family name printed on the invitation, followed by having you remove your mask to confirm my suspicions. Trust me. Now that your mask is back in place, no one will have the slightest inkling of your identity unless you choose to divulge it." He gestured to a large white door with a gold handle and filigree trim. "Ready?"

Less now than even a few moments before. But she was here and she intended to make the effort worth it. "Ready."

He swung open the door. Music and laughter

spilled into the marble vestibule as a blur of costumed merrymakers swirled past.

As she took a hesitant step over the threshold, the doorkeeper called out, "Lady X!"

Startled, she sent him a sharp glance over her shoulder.

"Don't worry," he murmured. "All the ladies are Lady X."

"Lady X!" the crowd cheered in response to the doorkeeper's bellow.

Within seconds, the door to the vestibule had closed and a court jester now hovered in its place, balancing a tray of brimming champagne glasses on his outstretched arm.

Camellia resisted the urge to fortify herself with the contents of the entire tray and limited herself to clutching a single frothy glass instead.

This large, open chamber was not the main ballroom, but music from the nearby orchestra nonetheless bounced like refracted light across the crystal chandeliers and reverberated up through the marble floor. A thrill hummed through her veins at the whirl of masked revelers and the thrum of music.

Now she knew what the Grenville musicales had been missing... Everything! Gold filigreed arched doorways led from the current chamber to several others and beyond. Singing here would be like performing at an opera. And, of course, just as scandalous.

To her right was the orchestra, where a crush of dashing lords and ladies danced far too close for propriety. No one seemed to care. The theme of the night seemed to be indulging any desire that crossed one's mind. A gasp choked in Camellia's throat as she spied more than one masked lord steal a kiss from his lady as they twirled about the dance floor in time to the music.

To the left was a card room, where elegant women wagered right alongside the men. A few of the ladies were even perched on their gentlemen's laps! On the other side were smaller, more intimate rooms, with far less lighting, and... beds? Camellia couldn't tell if her pulse skipped from shock or excitement. One of the doors swung shut before she caught anything more than the briefest glimmer of the interior of the chamber.

To either side of the current chamber were slender staircases, leading to a narrow promenade circumnavigating what would have been the second floor, and giving a bird's eye view to the proceedings below. Glass-windowed doors seemed to open onto a balcony overlooking the rear garden.

At the rear of the chamber beneath the second story promenade, several wide carved doors spilled out onto some sort of stone courtyard, where more waiters in court jester costumes dispensed glass after glass of champagne to the fashionable sophisticates laughing and flirting beneath the stars.

Camellia gulped down the rest of her champagne and returned the empty glass to a passing tray without selecting another. She didn't dare!

This seemed like the sort of wicked wonderland where the wisest course of action would be to keep one's head.

Everything about the masquerade was exhilarating. The sounds, the scents, the colors. The knowledge that no one recognized anyone else, and if she chose to waltz too closely or allow a masked stranger to steal a kiss, no one would ever know. Her blood raced.

She took a deep breath and stepped into the jostling, joyous crowd, intending to slip through to the rear for a look at the duke's garden. She barely traversed a few yards through the chamber when the vestibule door swung open behind her.

The doorkeeper's voice rang out. "Lord and Lady X!"

"Lord and Lady X!" the crowd roared back, welcoming the anonymous newcomers with a lift of their glasses and a hearty cheer.

She grinned despite herself. It was impossible not to get caught up in the revelry. One couldn't help but cheer with the crowd as each Lord or Lady X's name was called. It was ridiculous, infectious, marvelous *fun*.

Another court jester with a tray of champagne appeared from out of nowhere. Nearly all the offered glasses were gone within seconds. Camellia found herself reaching for the last one—until her fingers were intercepted by a man in a leering Venetian mask with tiny black eyes and a monstrous hooked nose. He tugged her to him too sharply and she nearly stumbled.

"Lady X," he said as he caressed the back of her hand. "Just the woman I've been waiting for."

"I'm not…" she began, but broke off her stammered denial. She wasn't what? Wasn't Lady X? Of course she was. They all were.

Camellia tensed. She had no intention to be anywhere near someone who would pull her bodily to him with no regard for her own wishes. She would have plenty of that with her future husband. She would not stand for it from a stranger.

"There, now that we've met," the man continued, his expression impossible to read behind the protruding papier-mâché of his mask. "Shall we find a cozier chamber in which to get to know each other more fully?"

"No." She tried to tug her fingers from his grasp. "Let me go."

"I think not." He tightened his hold. "Why would you wish to go somewhere else? You've only just arrived."

"Because she's waiting for me," growled a smooth voice laced with controlled power from somewhere just behind her.

"My apologies, Lord X." The papier-mâché released Camellia's fingers with a curl of his lip. "I did not realize the lady had been claimed."

"She claimed me." A strong hand lightly touched the small of her back. "The lady knows her own mind. I believe you asked me to steal a kiss atop the promenade, did you not?"

Camellia hesitated only briefly. She would not

be granting any kisses, but there was nothing she wanted more than to be one story higher, viewing the merry crush from a safe distance. "What took you so long, darling?"

She turned, expecting to be confronted with another terrifying mask with overlarge features. Instead, a tall, refined gentleman with a trim, muscular form gazed back at her from behind a simple black mask. In fact, other than the golden blond of his hair and the stark white of his cravat, he was dressed in smooth, impeccable black from his boots to his shoulders. Far from monstrous, he appeared dashing and mysterious.

"I almost didn't make it," he said cryptically as he offered his arm. "But now I am glad I did."

So was she.

Camellia's cheeks burned behind the safety of her blue-plumed mask as her masked rescuer led her toward the closest staircase. The crowd parted around him with every step, as if they too sensed his restrained power. She had to ignore the feel of hard muscle beneath her gloved fingers, the implied promise of a stolen kiss in their future, lest she trip over her own feet and bring them both crashing down the stairs before they even reached the top.

Not that she wanted a kiss. The idea terrified her as much as thrilled her. And the fact that she'd been present at the masquerade for less than half an hour, and had already been fought over by two men... She grinned to herself.

Bryony was going to be *so* vexed that Camellia had taken her place.

At the top of the stairs, the black masked gentleman once again proffered his arm. She took it. He led her not for a stroll about the interior promenade, but rather through one of the open doorways overlooking the garden.

The anonymous revelers out on the shadowed balcony were too involved in their own intimate conversations and scandalous embraces to notice two silent newcomers cross behind them to a series of Chinese folding screens.

Low murmurs could be heard behind the first of the delicately painted dividers. Soft giggles emanated from the second. The third, however, was silent, and Camellia found herself being whisked behind a cherry blossom screen into utter darkness.

Her breath caught in fear. He *was* going to kiss her. She had not been rescued, but abducted. This was it. Gooseflesh prickled down her bare arms. Should she scream? Run? Let him do it—and then ram her knee where her brother had taught her? Her heart pounded loud enough to drown out all the other sounds of the night.

Slowly, her eyes adjusted to the dark. The masked man was not leering at her suggestively, but lounging in one of two carved wooden chairs, his head lolling back against the edge as if he were utterly exhausted.

"Did you know that man?" he asked, his voice low.

She shook her head before realizing he could not see her doing so. His mask was tilted upward toward the faint spray of stars above the folding screen.

"No." She bit her lip with indecision. Should she sneak away? Or sit beside him? "I've never met him. As far as I know. With that carnival mask… he could be anyone."

"Not anyone." Her rescuer stretched out his legs and tucked his laced hands behind his head. "Masquerades are for privacy, not unwanted pressure. I'll inform Fair—the doorkeeper, that is. He'll know who it was. And Lambley will take care of the blackguard once and for all. He shan't return."

She swallowed. The promise was both reassuring… and ominous. Her skin prickled. She had not actually come to any harm—had been in the center of an impressively crowded room, in fact—but this gentleman was affirming what she had suspected at the time. She had been right to be afraid. Any "gentleman" who grabbed a lady's unwilling hand and refused to let go in public… what might he have done if he'd managed to corner her somewhere private?

Certainly not throw himself into a cushioned balcony chair to peacefully watch the stars. She let herself relax slightly. Now that she no longer feared having to thwart unwanted attentions, she was not quite certain what to do. Walk away… or stay?

"I don't believe we have met," her rescuer said

presently. His mask tilted toward where she stood. "I am Lord X. It is a pleasure to make your acquaintance."

He did not stand, as would have been required behavior in a proper ballroom. But they were far, far away from the land of propriety. The rules were different here. She would simply have to learn them.

She took the empty seat adjacent to him and folded her hands primly in her lap. Her heart calmed. "Lady X."

"The honor is mine." He tilted his head. "Did you wish for me to ravish you, now that we are alone?"

Her pulse jumped at the bold question. Good heavens! How was she meant to respond to such a query? Her voice squeaked as she managed, "Not at the moment."

"Perfect." He returned his gaze to the stars. "It's so rare for me to be in public and to still be able to just *breathe*."

Although she understood what he meant, her lips curved at the phrasing. "You do not often breathe in public?"

"Not freely," he replied, his tone resigned. "Too much is expected of me. I must act a certain way, be a certain thing. It is as if I am a music box, forced to play a melody not of my making every time they wind me up to dance. Not for myself, but for the masses. They return because they love to hear the same tune over and over. No one considers what might be best for the box."

She stared at him in wonder. Not only were his words more poetic than she would ever have expected, not only did his choice of music for his metaphor speak directly to her soul, but also the sentiment itself was one she'd felt every moment of every day for as long as she could remember.

He might be a figurative music box, but for Camellia it was almost literal. She was a spinster, quite on the shelf. Pretty but dusty, and utterly forgotten—until it was time for the Grenville soirée musicale. Then, and only then, was she plucked from her shelf and placed on a stage.

Her winding mechanism was her sister on the violin, but the hands cranking the key belonged to her parents. They provided the score. She was expected to follow it.

So she sang. Not the songs of her choosing, nor the time or the place, but the arrangement her parents had designed years before. The same arrangement she and her siblings performed at every single musicale, because it had become what the Grenvilles were famous for. What their pampered, fashionable guests wanted to hear. A programmed melody, which sounded only when each tiny clockwork spring bounced dully in place.

Why would the masked gentleman have chosen such an apt metaphor?

"Do you know who I am?" she stammered.

His head tilted her way. "I haven't the least idea. Nor are we allowed to enquire. Lambley does not hesitate to revoke all future invitations to anyone who breaks his rules. No, Lady X. I am afraid our identities will forever remain a mystery."

Perfect. A strange peace settled over her. He didn't know and couldn't ask. She was simply an anonymous, masked lady in a clandestine corner of a private balcony with an anonymous, masked man.

Who felt precisely as she did. As if they were twin souls.

Foolish, of course.

Camellia did not believe in twin souls, nor would she expect to stumble over one amidst the bustle of a scandalous masquerade ball. Yet she rather liked this gentleman. For a brief moment, she had feared he had meant to violate her, and instead he had simply wanted to breathe. Somewhere he was not alone.

Later, when he had asked her if she wished for him to ravish her, she had interpreted the question not as a threat, but rather an offer. And that was all it was. An offer to appease *her* expectations, not a demand to force his own desires upon her.

The masquerade was a safer place than it looked, she realized slowly. With the exception of the individual who would apparently be banned from these premises for his rudeness, every person under the duke's protection was free to do precisely as he or she pleased. Those who wished to dance, danced. Any debauched behavior was by mutual consent. Those who wished to wager, to eat, to drink, to flirt with strangers, to explore the garden, to do nothing more than sit back and stare up at the stars... Here, tonight, they could.

Masquerades weren't about scandal. They were about *choice*.

"The party is lovely," she ventured. "Is this your first time?"

Her rescuer chuckled. "I was at the very first one. Before anyone ever suspected how large these gatherings would one day become. Lambley is a personal friend."

She tilted her head. One might think that admitting to a personal friendship with a duke might give insight into one's secret identity, but when the duke in question was the sort to throw a party open to all walks of life from all classes and demimondes, provided the guests followed a few simple rules... The gentleman seated at Camellia's side could still be absolutely anyone. A footman. A soldier. A prince.

Despite not sharing his name, the man's open, easy manner and frank, honest answers made her feel as though she could quickly get to know him better than any of the frequent guests to her family musicales.

Unlike masquerades, her family musicales were not about choice. They were about doing what one was told. Performing as expected.

Afterwards, men did not fight over Camellia's hand. They did not speak to her at all. No one did. Although she remained on the stage, once the music was over, their interest in her vanished.

She no longer tried. Their attention only lasted as long as her song.

Until now.

She gazed through her lashes at the gentleman at her side. He showed no sign of wishing to quit her company. Or of stealing any kisses. Her cheeks heated at the oddly intriguing idea. Now that she knew the promise had only been a pretext, that he wouldn't kiss her unless she wanted him to… She almost wished he would.

When else would she have such a chance?

"So. Lord X." She fished for something to say. "Do you come here often?"

"Every single one," he answered without hesitation. "Sometimes I dance and sometimes I don't. It depends on how the week has gone. Sometimes I feel like drinking champagne at the center of the most fashionable mob in London, and sometimes I lean against the wainscoting and take it all in from a distance. Sometimes I meet a beautiful woman…" A crooked smile bloomed beneath his mask. "But this is the first time I've sneaked away with one to watch the stars. Are you terribly bored?"

She shook her head. Terribly charmed would be more accurate. She loved the stars; loved nature. Her sisters accused her of never leaving the house, but that wasn't true. She simply didn't attend high society routs. That wasn't where she felt at home.

While her sisters were off at this soirée or that tea salon, Camellia escaped to her favorite private stretch of land deep in the undeveloped section of Hyde Park's many acres, where she loved to climb up on her favorite rock and listen to the sound of the river.

She supposed she felt about the rippling water and the countless leaves overhead the way the man at her side felt about the stars. Sometimes, feeling small, feeling insignificant, actually made her feel more connected to the universe. Everything played its part, and gave her the strength to play hers.

"I don't blame you," she said. "I see how a masquerade could be... freeing."

He stared at her in silence for a moment, as if debating whether to speak. "Would you think me foolish if I told you that only when I'm disguised beneath a mask, can I ever truly be myself?"

"I would think you looked inside my own heart," she answered matter-of-factly.

Was she ever truly herself? Or was she always Camellia, the good girl, the wallflower, the dutiful daughter? She bit her lip at her own uncertainty. Was she boringly good because she wanted to be? Or simply because no one expected anything else from her?

She suddenly wished he hadn't merely *pretended* to want to kiss her. It would have been her first time. She might have liked the experience. With him, anyway. Her skin warmed. There would have been no strings, no scandal, no expectation of marriage. Just a kiss between two people who shared a brief connection beneath the stars.

He was right. Her mask was more than artistic blue feathers. It was freedom. For as long as she was wearing it, she would do and say as she pleased. And if he changed his mind about wanting to kiss her, decided to ask again...

Tonight, she'd let him.

CHAPTER 4

From behind the black-feathered mask keeping his identity safe, Michael gazed at the enchanting woman at his side.

She had thus far surprised him at every turn. That in itself was rare. Most of the females who attended the duke's masquerade balls fell into one of two categories.

The first type were the courtesans and demi-mondaines who had earned their fame and fortunes by dangling their sexuality before men who were more than eager to avail themselves of sensual favors.

The second type were the widows and dowagers and bored countesses and brazen debutantes who wished to *play* at being world-weary sensual creatures. A flirtatious dalliance, an anonymous seduction, or even a debauched night out with their own husbands… It was always a few hours' escapade to pretend to be someone they were not.

Not to finally be who they actually *were*.

Michael had never before admitted that the real reason he came to the masquerades was not for the wine or the women or the salacious possibilities, but because it was the one public place where nothing at all was required or expected of him.

Anywhere else, he was rakish Lord Wainwright, inveterate bachelor, well-heeled earl, accomplished flirt. Even when he was not trying to be any of those things, every word he spoke was interpreted as a double entendre, every glance perceived as an invitation to the bedchamber, every smile a promise of seduction.

Last night's caricature was proof positive of his predicament. Michael's friends might find it a merry jest that he need not do anything more than exist at the periphery of a gaggle of maidens for them to tumble over themselves in a fit of the vapors, but the truth was, such constant *on*-ness was more than exhausting. It made having an actual conversation with any member of the fairer sex utterly impossible.

Here, it was different. Tonight especially. Michael had not been certain if the man in the Venetian mask had been bothering the woman in blue—some couples enjoyed "meeting" their partner at the masquerade using assumed roles. When he intervened on her behalf... she had hesitated.

Hesitated! He shook his head wryly. Such a thing would have never occurred in a public ballroom with their masks off. Lady X would have swooned into his open arms, followed by—no, not even that. His smile was self-mocking. Without his mask, he wouldn't have been able to rescue anyone. They would never have spoken.

The moment he walked into a room, he changed its makeup with his mere presence. The blackguards would wait until he quit the chamber before resuming their unwanted advances. The sillier debutantes would grapple for their smelling salts and the more experienced women would flutter coquettish eyes at him over their painted fans to broadcast their interest.

The woman in blue had done none of those things. She had gone with him because he was the lesser evil, not because he possessed a title or a bottomless pocketbook or a handsome face. She didn't even know if he *had* a handsome face, because a winged black mask covered the top half of it.

Nor had she left, now that she was here. There was a moment where he'd thought she might fly away. When he'd taken his seat and she had not taken hers. When she'd told him no, she was not particularly interested in him ravishing her. She was the first woman to have ever said no. Yet she'd stayed.

His world was upside down.

Everyone who entered these doors did so for wanton reasons. Perhaps they were here with a spouse, or to cuckold one, or perhaps they sought adventure, or a break in a long line of paid assignations. Here, he might not be the infamous Lord

Wainwright, but he was still a man, and that was often the sum of the attending ladies' requirements.

Inside or outside these walls, these women didn't care about *him*. They cared about what he could give them. Those who knew his name were after anything from a waltz to the role of countess. Those who knew him only as Lord X simply wished for a night of mutual pleasure.

Up until now, it had been enough. He had wanted the same things. To be able to indulge desires without involving banns and vicars. This was the place.

One of a masquerade's many advantages was that there were no "innocents" present. Michael had unquestionably earned his rakehell reputation, but he had never despoiled any virgins. All of his conquests had been experienced women who loved the thrill of the chase as much as he did.

So what had brought the lady in blue to such a soirée? He turned toward her.

"Do *you* come here often?" He tried not to display how interested he was in the answer. In everything about her.

She touched one of her earrings and shook her head. "This is my first time."

Good. He was pleased that he had also been the first to whisk her away. It felt like he'd been given a treat. Secret access to a special delicacy, one that no one else even knew existed.

"Tell me about yourself," he urged impulsively.

He shouldn't have. The question wasn't the same as the forbidden "What's your name?" but it was dangerous enough that they were both better off if she didn't answer. Yet he wished she would.

She sidestepped the question. "With your love of music, I imagine you must be a patron of the arts."

Ah. His complaint about how tough it was to be a rich, popular earl. Michael had felt embarrassed even saying the words. "I try to be."

He was fortunate. He *knew* he was fortunate. What was there to complain about? Other men *wished* they had Michael's problems. Too many women, too much money, an earldom. What they didn't realize was how often he wished he had *their* problems.

Lord Hawkridge might be penniless, but at least he knew his friends weren't out for his money. Gideon owned a gaming parlor, not an earldom, but at least he knew women were flirting with *him*, not his title.

The once-respectable Anthony Fairfax had been reduced to earning his keep as a paid door-keeper at Lambley's masquerades, but every night he went home to a wife who loved him. What might that be like?

One should not dwell on the fortunes of others, Michael reminded himself. Especially not tonight. He had found the one person of the entire company who was more interested in keeping her clothes on than taking them off. To her, Lord X possessed more than a body. He also possessed a mind. He should endeavor to use it.

"Do you own a music box?" she asked him.

"I do not," he answered. "But I have visited a music box factory in Switzerland that opened two years past, and I own several other musical instruments."

"Do you?" She leaned forward in obvious interest. "Which ones?"

Exclusively harps, but he could not tell her so without giving away his identity. "Lord Wainwright's harp room" was almost as scandalous as the duke's masquerades, and for much the same reason. It was allegedly the site of so much debauchery, a bawdyhouse madam would blush to enter.

Only a few friends had ever even seen Michael's secret trove of musical instruments, so he was not entirely certain how its existence had become public knowledge—or why something as innocuous as *harps* had been turned into code for bacchanalia.

There were a few naked angels painted into the fresco on the ceiling, but good God. Sprightly cherubs were a far cry from saturnalia. Nonetheless, collecting harps was not something he could admit to. Not if he wanted the lady in blue to keep treating him like a man, rather than a caricature. Particularly if she'd seen the printed etchings of what the local artists imagined occurred inside Michael's infamous harp room.

"String instruments," he said instead, and hoped it would suffice. "I have several."

She beamed at him. "That is lovely. I love music, too. I assume you play?"

He blinked. No one had ever assumed he played before. Or had any particular talent outside of the bedchamber. No one cared to know about his love of travel, of nature, of the stars. For the first time… someone was interested in him as a person.

Unfortunately, in this particular case, the gossiping masses were right. He could not boast musical talent, or even rudimentary knowledge. And he feared his ignorance on the matter would not impress the lady in blue.

"I am afraid I do not play." The back of his neck heated.

She tilted her head. "Why not?"

"I have never thought of it."

The answer would not win him any favors, but it was honest. He collected harps for emotional reasons, not musical ones.

His mother had been the one who played. When she'd died, Michael has been unable to part with her collection. The opposite, in fact. He'd begun to add to it. One harp for every year without his parents. In a foolish sort of way, it made him feel as if they were still with him. If only in one room of the house.

The lady in blue leaned back in her chair. "And now that you have thought about it? Playing, I mean?"

He stared back at her. The topic had been broached, but he wouldn't say he'd *thought* about it, even now. The harps weren't his. They were his mother's. Besides, an earl had no business plinking at harp strings. Not if the earl in question was Lord Wainwright. He could not allow the caricaturists to use his mother's legacy as fodder for ridicule.

"Inappropriate behavior for a man of my station," he replied instead.

It was a slightly less honest answer than all the others he'd given her, and he could not help but feel a twinge of shame over how pompous it made him sound. The last thing he wanted was to ruin this moment with Lady X. He was still behind his mask. He could be himself with her. Or at least honest.

So he forced himself to add, "It would cause as much stir as a debutante doubling as an opera singer."

He'd meant the comparison as a jest.

She didn't laugh.

He changed the subject to cover his misstep. "Do you have any siblings?"

Her face lit up. No, not her face—her entire manner. As if the very mention of her siblings brightened her world.

"I do," she said. "Several. They drive me mad, but I wouldn't have it any other way."

He leaned forward. "You're very close?"

"The best of friends. There's nothing we wouldn't do for each other." She smiled as if recalling a fond memory. "How about you? Do you have any siblings?"

"Not a one," he admitted. "But you're making me wish I did. I don't suppose you have a spare to loan me?"

"I couldn't bear to part with any of them," she answered cheerfully. "I am afraid you'll have to envy me from afar."

Michael blinked. He hadn't said he was *jealous* of her siblings. But the fact that she took for granted that her relationship with them was something worth envying… He tilted toward her. The lady in blue was fascinating indeed.

"You look splendid tonight," he said presently. It was true. He'd been shamelessly staring for almost an hour, but the moonless night did little to penetrate the shadow of the privacy screen.

He wished he could see her more clearly. There had been more light in the chandelier-filled chamber, but also exponentially more chaos. Before charging in to rescue her, he had glimpsed little more than her dark hair and pink lips. Their flight up the stairs had allowed him to recognize her beauty.

"It's… a new gown." She rose to her feet and spun in a circle, as if to display her womanly advantages as much as mock them. "Thank you."

He smiled, more charmed than he cared to admit. "The blue looks especially fetching on you."

"Not *blue*," she corrected, her voice teasing. "Sapphire. My sister informs me that mere 'blue' is dreadfully common."

"You look like a princess," he assured her as he rose to his feet to join her. "A somewhat naughty princess with a plunging neckline and a mysterious plumed mask, but unquestionably a princess."

She burst out laughing. "You're definitely a prince. Your manners are impeccable. I don't suppose you have a castle nearby?"

He rather wished he did. "Would you want to go there?"

"No," she said simply. "I'm enjoying tonight, just as it is. I do not want it to stop." Her tone turned wistful. "I won't be back."

His frown was genuine. "Why not? I thought you were enjoying yourself."

"I am. But you were right about the roles we're required to play. I'll have some new responsibilities in about a month, and will no longer be at liberty to attend soirées." Her smile was lopsided. "Not even anonymously."

He leaned forward, suddenly desperate not to lose her. "A month is more time than you might think. The Season is underway, and this time Lambley is holding a masquerade every week rather than every fortnight." He took her hands in his. "Whatever your responsibilities are, you still have three more opportunities to put on a mask and escape for a few hours."

Her lips quirked. "I should come back for champagne delivered by court jesters?"

"No," he said softly. "Come back for me."

She didn't remove her hands from his. Instead, she tilted her face up toward him, her expression a mystery behind her silver mask. "I don't have an invitation."

He lowered his lips until there was nothing between them but shadow and the promise of far more. "I'll make certain you get one."

"How?" She didn't move away.

He could almost taste the champagne sweetness of her breath. Wished he could taste her lips. Hoped this meant she would return. "I'll request a special guest invitation and have Lambley notify the doorkeeper. The keyword will be 'sapphire.' Like your dress."

Her tone was light. "You like my gown, then?"

Yes. Worse. Michael was beginning to like the woman inside it even better.

"Say you'll come," he demanded. He was blocking the starlight, could no longer see her, but every inch of his body was almost painfully aware of every inch of hers. The scooped neckline he'd admired so much was close enough to brush beneath his cravat. Her skirt swirled against his boots, his thighs. Her lips were close enough to kiss.

"Why should I?" she whispered.

He covered her mouth with his and answered with a kiss. Heat. Heaven. She should come back because they both wanted to. Wanted this. The wind in their hair and the stars overhead. His mouth on hers. Nothing between them but the night. A kiss sweeter than any he'd ever known.

At last, he forced himself to pull away.

"Is that a yes?" he asked, his voice rough with passion.

Rather than reply, she spun out of his arms and slipped behind the painted screen. "See you next time, Lord X."

"*Wait.*" He dashed around the divider, but she was nowhere to be seen. Not on the balcony, not behind any of the other screens.

He hurried to the stairs just in time to see a flash of blue slip through an exit leading toward the main road. His throat went dry at the thought of losing her so soon after finding her. With a muttered curse, he raced down the stairs and through the crowd and burst out of the masquerade into the chill, crisp night just as the clocktower bells tolled midnight.

Rows of carriages stretched from one side of the ducal estate to the other. None were in motion. There was no telltale swirl of blue silk, no sign of Lady X anywhere. She had vanished without a trace.

It was as if his princess had disappeared by magic.

CHAPTER 5

One of the few positive sides to being stuck in a moving carriage with one's mother and both sisters was that, as the eldest, Camellia's rank afforded her one half of the coveted front-facing seat. The converse, of course, meant that she had to share that seat with her mother, who could not stop talking about Camellia's impending marriage to mature, respectable, lonely-country-home-somewhere-near-the-Scottish-border Mr. Bost.

"Have you thought about what you might wear?" Mother chirped. "Puffed sleeves emphasize your youthfulness, but perhaps that is the wrong tack to take with a—"

"Mature?" Camellia asked dryly.

"Respectable?" Dahlia put in.

"Not quite Scottish?" Bryony whispered.

"—gentleman like Mr. Bost." Mother tapped her chin in deep thought. "Long sleeves, then.

The weather's frightful enough, I daresay you'll be more comfortable than your sisters."

"We won't be wearing long sleeves, too?" asked Dahlia. "Won't that offend Mr. Bost's gentlemanly sensibilities?"

"He cannot take offense," Bryony assured her. "We're less mature than Cam. And less respectable."

Dahlia brightened. "Very true! Everyone knows you're a dreadful hoyden."

Bryony shook a finger. "Everyone also knows that *you* are a sharp-tongued headmistress, intent on beating the 'hoyden' out of your poor, misunderstood wards."

"I need not *strike* them," Dahlia protested, clutching a hand to her chest in mock affront. "Threaten to revoke lemon cake privileges and they all turn into perfect angels."

"Withholding food from destitute children!" Bryony gasped in exaggerated outrage. "Good heavens, we are far less mature than Cam. Long sleeves for us would be *unthinkable*."

"Without question," Dahlia agreed. "To make matters worse, as the eldest, Cam out-spinsters me by almost a full year. Obviously she cannot be seen in puffed sleeves at such an advanced age."

"Perhaps woolen sleeves are best. Think of the frightful weather!" Bryony patted Camellia's knee. "What if the dear old heart should catch cold and be unable to continue the ceremony?"

Camellia returned her smile through clenched teeth.

"Not wool. *Silk*," Mother decided with a sharp nod. "It's the only choice. We'll have the wedding ensemble made on Bond Street. In fact, we all deserve new gowns, do we not? I'll have your father increase our spending credit between now and the wedding."

"Wonderful," Camellia said, unable to keep the bleakness from her voice. "I can't wait."

After being kissed by Lord X, the thought of a lifetime with a perfectly respectable, perfectly normal, perfectly boring gentleman like Mr. Bost was the last thing she desired. Yet it was all she would ever have.

"One can hardly blame you, darling." Mother patted Camellia's knee, seemingly unaware that her youngest daughter had also just done so in satire of the maternal habit. "I, too, had despaired of you ever finding a match. Mr. Bost is not only a—"

"Mature?" Dahlia asked.

"Respectable?" Bryony added innocently.

Camellia covered her face with her hands.

"—gentleman," Mother continued, "he will be able to keep you in a great deal of comfort. You shall not want for a thing from the very moment the wedding concludes until your dying day."

"Your dying day!" Bryony thumped Camellia's knee with excessive force. "Won't *that* be exciting?"

"I can't wait," Camellia repeated, with more feeling this time.

Mother let out a little sigh of happiness. "I had

hoped for a title, but honestly, who could complain about a mature, respectable gentleman like our kind Mr. Bost? One can only hope one's other daughters receive offers even half as fine as their elder sister's. Now that it's seemly to receive them, of course."

Camellia pressed her lips together at the slight.

Until the elder sister was married, or at least betrothed, younger sisters could not be considered for such a step. The wedding with Mr. Bost would be as much for their benefit as it ostensibly was for hers. More so, in fact. The younger two were more outgoing, more likely to attract suitors—if only their wallflower sister wasn't obstructing their chances. That was the real reason Camellia was going through with this. It was the right thing to do for the people she loved.

That, and the fact that Mother was right. There had been no other offers. If Camellia did not marry Mr. Bost, she would doom all three sisters to die spinsters. So as much as she might wish to wed someone she *wanted* rather than someone she ought... There was no choice, and Camellia knew it.

She had meant every word when she'd told Lord X there wasn't anything she and her siblings wouldn't do for each other. Bryony had promised she would rather die a spinster than consign Camellia to a husband she did not love. Dahlia had declared herself married to the administration of her school, with no intention of losing all ownership and control over her life's work by becoming a wife.

Camellia swallowed her guilt. That was easy enough for them to say now. Neither of them had ever been kissed, much less fallen in love. But if she turned down the opportunity to marry Bost and one of her sisters *did* meet a love match... Camellia would never forgive herself if they lost the opportunity because their parents refused to consider offers until the eldest daughter was safely wed.

After all—adhering to protocol was only proper. A trait her parents prized above all other considerations.

She let her head fall back against the rear wall of the carriage in resignation. Her sisters didn't realize it, but their tendency to rebel was the primary reason Camellia did not. The worse they acted, the better she felt obligated to behave. Some level of balance had to be kept in the home, and if it could only be achieved by Camellia being proper and unobtrusive enough to counteract the effects of her siblings, then so be it.

Her parents were good people who wanted the best for their children. Who wouldn't? Their eldest son Heath was less of a concern simply because he was male. He could wed a debutante decades from now when he was as mature and respectable as Mr. Bost, and no one would blink an eye.

Girls, on the other hand, needed to be married off young, lest they become burdens on their family. Camellia was already six-and-twenty, which meant all three sisters were becoming long in the tooth. If anything, she should be flattered anyone would settle for her at all.

Inevitably, her thoughts returned to the masquerade, as they had done from the moment she left.

Lord X hadn't appeared to be settling for a spinster. She had captured his attention—*she*, in a palatial residence brimming with glamorous women!—and he had absconded with her to the balcony because he wished to. Not because he was in want of a dowry or because she was the elder sister and therefore first in line. She might have been anyone. A countess, a mistress, a governess. And he'd chosen her.

Lambley's masked balls were the antithesis of Almack's assembly rooms. The masquerade was no marriage market. The longest its merrymakers expected to stay together were the short hours from ten to dawn. As to debutantes, she doubted there had been any. From the sound of the duke's rules and the scrutiny of his doorkeeper, Camellia was likely the youngest reveler in attendance.

It was not a place for respectable ladies—and definitely not for Camellia. She well knew she'd be betrothed in a month. The last thing she should do was tie herself up in even more knots by going back in search of a man whose name she would never know.

And yet, from the moment Lord X had asked her to return… she'd known she would.

After all, if she was doomed to spend the rest of her life in a loveless relationship in Northumberland hundreds of miles from her family… then by God she was going to waltz with a handsome stranger for once in her life first.

"Bryony, I do wish your hair would hold a bit more of its curl." Mother leaned forward to twist one of Bryony's limp tendrils about her finger. "It's so embarrassing when my daughter's ringlets are lopsided."

As usual, Bryony suffered through this indignity without so much as an eye roll. When their mother got an idea into her head, there was absolutely nothing that could stop her. "Aren't we going home? No one will even see my hair. But I shall promise to take an iron to it anyway, if the thought of me seated in my private chambers with lopsided curls will give you palpitations."

"We are not going directly home." Mother untwisted the first ringlet from her finger and reached for a second. "I am too excited about Camellia's upcoming nuptials to retire early, aren't you?"

Bryony and Camellia exchanged long-suffering glances.

Dahlia looked up from the thick book in her lap. "If we are not headed home, then where are we going?"

"Why, to the Earl of Wainwright's evening soirée, of course."

"Stop the carriage." Dahlia slammed her book closed. All color drained from her countenance.

"I am not stepping foot on that self-important cretin's property and neither are any of you."

"We must and we shall." Mother sent her a stern look. "One should always accept any invitation sealed with a crest from the peerage."

"The only invitation I'll accept from that blackguard is to meet with pistols at dawn," Dahlia said darkly.

"You are so funny, darling." Mother poked Dahlia's nose with the tip of a gloved finger before returning her attention to Bryony's hair. "Fudge. That's as good as we're going to get without an iron. It will simply have to do."

"I'm not going," Dahlia repeated. "He is the worst of his kind."

Mother sighed. "Pinch your cheeks for color and try not to be petulant in front of the earl. We're almost there."

"I'll take her home," Camellia offered. "Dahlia and I can… plan my wedding. It'll be her turn next, so I am sure she will not want to miss any of the details."

"I can help," Bryony said quickly. "My lopsided curls are an embarrassment to this family. My time would be much better spent helping Cam choose the perfect location for her betrothal announcement."

"You are all meeting the earl." Mother's tone brooked no argument. "Besides, I've already chosen the time and location for the betrothal announcement."

"You have?" Camellia's stomach sank. "When? Where?"

"At the next soirée musicale, of course. It's going to be splendid!" Mother clasped her hands to her chest with an excited wiggle. "The entire ton will be present to hear you sing. Therefore, to ensure nobody misses the moment, you shall announce the betrothal immediately after the last note."

"Me?" Camellia choked. "Shouldn't Father make the announcement? Or Mr. Bost?"

"They won't be on stage. *You* will be," Mother pointed out reasonably. "Do be practical."

The carriage pulled to a stop.

"I shan't speak a word to him," Dahlia warned. She held up the tome she'd been studying. "This is *Debrett's*. My one remaining hope. If that blackguard poisons the last few potential donors away from helping the school before I have an opportunity to explain the impact each pound makes on a worthy life—"

"I'll tell you what I told Bryony," Mother interrupted, her face stern. "If women were meant to have businesses, it would be legal for wives to own one. Stop this rubbish. If you wish to donate to worthy causes, fine. Marry well, and spend your husband's riches as you please. *That* is what woman's duty is about."

Camellia exchanged an appalled glance with her sister.

Bryony leaned forward. "And I'll tell you what

I told Mother when she tried that poppycock with me. I said—"

"You will *not* repeat such language, now or ever," Mother snapped. "Take your reticules, leave your foolish books, and go and rub shoulders with people who are more important than a mere baroness and her ungrateful chits."

All three sisters piled out of the carriage in communal silence and filed after their mother, not as chastised little ducklings, but like condemned inmates being forced to the gallows.

Camellia supposed her wedding march would not be dissimilar. Perhaps she ought to get used to the sensation.

To Lord Wainwright's credit—or rather, to the credit of the conceited earl's many generations of rich ancestors—everything about his residence was lush and beautiful. Three stately stories rose up from the expansive garden surrounding them. Neat rows of spotless glass windows decorated each floor. Rather than gargoyles, tiny cherubic angels adorned the waterspouts along the roof.

"Ironic," Dahlia muttered.

Camellia couldn't help but agree. Even if Lord Wainwright *hadn't* managed to defund her sister's school with a single thoughtless remark, the man could not be further from an angel. Though she and the earl had never crossed paths, his celebrated rakehell reputation was second to none.

If Lord Wainwright hadn't also possessed a title, women like Camellia's mother would not have dared allow their daughters anywhere near him.

She nearly choked as she suddenly realized that must be precisely her mother's plan. Now that Camellia was all but betrothed, why not matchmake the second daughter with society's most eligible bachelor?

Unfortunately for Mother, Dahlia was far more disposed to enacting vengeance than ensnaring the earl's hand. It might have been wiser for Dahlia to wait in the carriage after all.

"Lady Grenville," the butler called out. "Miss Grenville, Miss Dahlia Grenville, and Miss Bryony Grenville."

At the sound of their names, Camellia stepped across the threshold into a world of opulence and splendor.

Luxurious carpets stretched across the center of every floor. Candles glittered in crystal chandeliers overhead. Silk wallpaper and shiny wainscoting covered each room. Intricate molding of brilliant white lined every ceiling. Sumptuous satins, gold filigree, delicately carved furniture... The place was a palace.

Although Camellia would not dare confess her admiration to her sister, she had never seen such a gorgeous home in all her life. Even without a party for diversion, she would be delighted to walk the corridors just to sigh in contentment at so much beauty.

Mother whacked Dahlia's spine with her

painted fan. "Correct your posture, please. A lady does not slump."

"Where are Father and Heath?" Dahlia growled as she straightened her spine. "Off at a gentlemen's club? Why do they always get to miss the fun?"

"Worse," Camellia whispered back grimly. "This is your circus. Mother means to matchmake you to Wainwright."

Dahlia paled. "Please be bamming me. Tell her I'm ruined. Tell her I've fallen in love with a stable boy."

"I doubt that would sway her. She'd pack you off with your own version of Bost before she'd let you sully the Grenville name with scandal."

Dahlia shuddered. "Luckily for everyone but Mother, a wife is the last thing Wainwright is in the market for. I've had blinks that lasted longer than the amount of time he spends with any given woman. If he notices our presence, he'll forget us the moment he turns away."

"He is like a goldfish," Bryony agreed. "A rakish, handsome, arrogant goldfish. Who is swimming up behind you as we speak."

Camellia snapped her spine straight and slowly turned to greet the face of the devil. Her throat dried at the sight.

He *did* look like an angel.

The caricaturists drew the famous earl as exaggeratedly tall, with a cravat of monstrous proportions and perfect ringlets so yellow they glowed like the sun.

The reality was considerably better.

His hair was neither glowing, nor composed of identical ringlets. Instead, his golden locks were combed into the current fashionable style that looked both careless and casual, but according to her brother Heath, took the better part of an hour to craft properly.

Or perhaps that was simply the curse of unruly Grenville hair.

Lord Wainwright's eyes were an entrancing hazel hue that changed color with every flicker of light from the chandeliers and invited the viewer to gaze upon them until she lost herself in the mystery. Brown. Gray. Green.

His nose was straight, his cheekbones breathtaking, his jaw as perfectly groomed as the rest of him. His cravat was blindingly white and carefully folded, but not so intricately as to label the wearer a fop. His waistcoat was a subtle gold, his wide shoulders ensconced in a handsome coat of charcoal gray, just soft enough a tone to make him stand out from the dandies in black and the peacocks in lime and puce.

But when he smiled... Heaven save them. Camellia's pulse fluttered as her cheeks flushed.

When Lord Wainwright's lips curved, every flame, every crystal chandelier, every gold filigree adorning the hand-painted walls paled next to the easy warmth of his smile and the answering sparkle in his fathomless green-brown-gray eyes.

"Did I swoon?" Bryony whispered. "I feel as though I swooned. If you didn't see me fall, I must have fainted on the inside. Someone pinch me, quick."

Dahlia kicked her in the ankle.

"Lady Grenville." Lord Wainwright sketched an elegant bow. "I shall be ever grateful that you accepted my humble invitation."

Mother tittered and dipped a simpering curtsey.

Good grief. It was all Camellia could do not to drop her face back into her palms. The caricaturists hadn't exaggerated one thing. Mother *never* tittered or dipped simpering curtseys. Incredible. Lord Wainwright's devastating effect on women was positively transcendent.

"This is my eldest daughter." Mother patted Camellia on the shoulder. "You would recognize her from our family musicales, but you have yet to attend one. We'd be deeply honored if you would. We are also hosting a dinner party next week if you would prefer to come to that."

"We are?" Bryony whispered. "Since when?"

"Since Mother decided to marry off the rest of you, too," Camellia whispered back.

"This is my second eldest." Ignoring Dahlia's ferocious scowls, Mother shoved her middle daughter forward. "Pay no attention to her current disposition. Dahlia has the megrims. She normally has a very pretty face. She also has naturally curly hair, fine sturdy bones, and would make any man a fine wife."

"It's as if we're auctioning a horse," Dahlia said through clenched teeth. "Should I whinny?"

"Not on my behalf." Lord Wainwright's gentle smile was reassuring. "I'm afraid some of the other guests frown on indoor whinnying, and we really ought not to disrupt their comfort. I shall simply assume that your bones are the sturdiest of the ton and your whinny the finest of any other young lady I've had the privilege to know."

Dahlia's answering glare didn't lessen in the slightest... but the look in Bryony's eyes could only be described as melting.

Camellia herself couldn't help but be impressed with the way the earl quickly and earnestly did his best to put them all at ease, from soothing Dahlia's understandably ruffled feathers to glossing over their mother's horrific behavior to making a silly jest to keep an extremely awkward moment from turning sour.

Yet she could not forgive him so easily for ruining the fund-raising chances for Dahlia's school. The unplanned words that tripped off his tongue to make each guest feel welcome came from the same thoughtless mechanism that caused him to interrupt a conversation with empty compliments capable of derailing months of planning and effort.

But she didn't think he *meant* to do it. She didn't even think he noticed. Already, Lord Wainwright was bowing to her mother and seamlessly gliding to the next clump of hopefuls, where he delivered his devastating smile and bestowed a few flattering words upon his tongue-tied guests before moving on to the next arrivals in line.

Camellia frowned. She wasn't certain that obliviousness negated the crime. The fact that he did not notice, that he interacted with others automatically rather than authentically, made her believe the caricaturists were right. He didn't bother hiding his superficial nature… and it didn't matter. Ladies melted like butter in his hand before he even opened his mouth.

"That went well, I think." Mother fanned her lace fichu with a painted fan. "I daresay he might attend our dinner party."

"He's not attending our dinner party," Dahlia said flatly. "He didn't even ask what day it was."

"An earl expects a formal invitation, of course. I shall send him one the moment we get home. And tomorrow as well, in case the first one gets lost." Mother tapped her chin. "Is three too many?"

"Three invitations are definitely too many." Camellia steered her mother away from the earl. "Goodness, is that not Lord and Lady Sheffield? I am sure they are dying for you to chat with them about the party."

"You're right, of course. I mustn't keep them waiting." Mother rushed toward the viscount and viscountess without a backward glance.

"Now what?" Camellia asked her sisters. Because she often kept to herself, Lord and Lady Sheffield were the only people she had recognized. On the other hand, Dahlia and Bryony both had busy social calendars and were likely to have several acquaintances in the crowd. "Should we mingle or stay close to the door?"

"We should stay away from the ratafia." Bryony tilted her head. "Lady Pettibone is guarding the refreshments. She's called 'the old dragon' for a reason. The lady can smite with a single glance."

"Let's find the retiring room," Camellia suggested. "If Mother asks where we went, Dahlia and I can say we were employing heroic efforts to un-droop your hair."

"I don't even like ringlets," Bryony sighed, but she followed them toward the nearest corridor.

Halfway down the hall, Dahlia grabbed their wrists and halted them just before they passed a crowded side room. "Shh, listen. They're talking about Wainwright."

The sounds spilling from the open door sounded more like a card game than scandal-broth. The clink of glasses and tinkle of betting fish blended with the murmur of male voices.

"Have you seen it?" asked one of the men.

"Seen what, the harps? Not yet. I hear they're all solid gold."

"They cannot all be solid gold, you imbecile. Who could lift a giant, solid gold harp?"

"Not you, obviously. God knows you've never won a single round at Jackson's."

"I'm mopping up the betting table with your pocketbook, am I not? That's trump. I win again."

A chair scooted across parquet. "Bugger all of you. I'm out."

"Go and find the harp room, coward. It's full of naked portraits. I hear they're even painted on the ceiling."

"Brilliant! Sort of a bawdy library for rakes who aren't bright enough to own books."

"I'd take it. Not all books have pictures."

A voice laughed. "The best ones do. Ever hear of etchings?"

"No one goes in the harp room to read, trust me. It's made for sin."

"I love the idea in theory but... Who would model for such a thing?"

"Probably your wife. All Wainwright has to do is crook a finger, and—"

Betting fish skittered across the floor as a scuffle broke out behind the wall.

Camellia's stomach turned. Had she just been thinking that poor Lord Wainwright's motives had possibly been misunderstood? His character was even worse than she'd previously suspected.

"Come with me." She steered her sisters back toward the main door. "We'll stay by the exit in full sight of the others until we can leave. I don't want anyone thinking we even know about Lord Wainwright's secret chamber of iniquity."

Or the earl's repulsive propensity to cuckold his own friends. She steeled her spine to hide her shudder.

He was a devil with an angel's face.

CHAPTER 6

*N*ow that Camellia had sworn to never again speak to Lord Wainwright—and now that, thanks to her mother, they'd suffered through the world's most awkward conversation—she saw the earl everywhere.

Camellia would not even be in town, were it not for her mother's insistence in mounting a formidable trousseau... and bedecking them all with new gowns in the process.

Everywhere she went, Lord Wainwright would come walking around the opposite corner. Bond Street, Oxford Street, Burlington Arcade, Saville Row, Floris on Jermyn Street. Camellia pressed her lips together in frustration. What the devil was the man doing? Outfitting his army of courtesans?

On a positive note, they did manage to avoid any further communication. Either Dahlia was right, and the earl had put them from his mind the moment he turned his back on them, or else his sense of self-preservation prevented him from so much as making eye contact while their mother was within a ten-block radius.

If only Camellia could escape her mother as easily.

For days, she had been trying without success to slip from the house undetected and flee to her secret refuge along the river.

She needed to think. To breathe. Her upcoming marriage loomed large in her mind, oppressing all other thoughts until all that was left was a wrenching despondency at the thought of being so far from her sisters. Northumberland was a world away. Four hundred miles might as well be four thousand.

From time to time, Camellia liked to escape for a few moments to refresh her inner spirit, but she could not imagine spending days, weeks, months at a time without seeing her family. What if Mr. Bost never wanted to return to London at all? What if years bled into decades and the next time she saw her sisters, their children were grown and Camellia had missed everything?

It was more than a fear. It was a distinct possibility. She would not be the first bride whose husband took her too far a distance for her to keep in touch with her family.

But she might be the first to die of a broken heart for it.

"Cam, are you listening?" came Dahlia's exasperated voice.

Camellia jerked her spine upright and focused

on her sister. She was so desperate not to lose her family that it was affecting her ability to concentrate while they were still here. She needed a restorative trip to her river rock now more than ever.

"I'm listening," she said. "You asked whether it's wise to take on a business partner, given the current state of financial uncertainty."

Dahlia nodded, her expression grateful. "Faith Digby is only slightly less of a wallflower than you are, but that means she has time for a big project. Because her family money comes from trade, Faith is looked down upon as mere *nouveau riche*. But *riche* is *riche*, I say. My school is in no position to turn away anyone's pennies. Although Faith has no Almack's voucher, she does have a few significant connections. She's a distant relative to none other than Lady Pettibone."

"The 'old dragon?'" Camellia asked skeptically. "Then why doesn't Miss Digby have an Almack's voucher?"

"*Distant* relative," Dahlia repeated. "Perhaps it's not much in the way of connections, but as to the rest of it… What do you think? Should I offer her half ownership of the school, in exchange for monetary patronage?"

A pang of nostalgia gripped Camellia by the heart. These were the conversations she'd miss the most. Lying in a chaise longue with one sister in the bay window and the other kicking up her stocking feet by the fire. Answering questions.

Being their sounding board. What would any of them do without each other?

"Well," she answered slowly. "I think Miss Digby sounds like a fine addition to the project. However, I think it unwise to make her a full partner before she has even stepped foot on the school grounds. Why don't you set some parameters that protect both of you? If, after three months, she still wishes to be a partner, and if, after three months, you still think her partnership is the right course for your school, then sign the contract."

Dahlia's eyes were desperate. "What if she says no?"

"To the contract?"

"To three months. If I do not make her a partner, and she loses interest altogether…"

Then the school would almost certainly be forced to close. Dahlia's destitute girls would be back on the streets.

Camellia leaned forward. "Then there should be two contracts. A temporary one, which spells out the agreement and the time limitations. For three months, she *has* to act in the best interest of the school. And *you* have to give her all the leeway and support she requires. After that, the two of you decide whether to make her temporary position permanent."

Dahlia launched from the window seat to envelop Camellia in a fierce embrace. "I knew you would have the answers. You always do. I'll miss you so much."

"I'll miss you too," Camellia said through the stinging in her throat. She hugged her sister back as if it were the last time. Every moment was precious. Already a week had vanished. A few more, and *she* would be the one with a permanent position she didn't want.

Dahlia kissed her cheek and dashed back to her traveling desk. "I shall write to her right now to let her know what we're thinking."

"Why don't you visit in person instead?" Camellia rose to her feet. "I'll accompany you partway."

"Brief respite at Hyde Park?" Dahlia asked with a knowing smile.

"Opposite of brief," Camellia agreed with a relieved sigh. "If we can leave with only one maid as chaperone, she can continue on with you after I alight." She slipped her father's old pocket watch into her reticule. "Come to fetch me exactly two hours after we part company."

Dahlia reached for her pelisse. "Perfect."

In no time at all, Camellia was striding through the park, first on well-trodden trails, then lesser-known paths, then an overgrown shortcut known only to her.

She emerged from a thicket into a wide expanse of bright green grass leading to a pristine river. Acres of virgin trees lined the other side. Their healthy profusion of fluttering leaves offered welcome shade from the dappled sun.

Wildflowers ran along the river's edge and into the woods, providing a touch of floral sweetness to the light, crisp breeze. A profound sense of contentment filled her at the sound of rippling water below, the song of birds overhead.

At long last, Camellia had returned to her hidden oasis.

She climbed up onto the large gray rock beside the river and lay back facing the sky. The weather was chill despite her pelisse, but wind-chapped cheeks were worth the chance to finally, fully relax.

A corner of her mouth curved at the irony. At home she enjoyed banging at the pianoforte and singing as loudly as she wished—her siblings were often even louder—but Camellia still needed to escape to the wild in order to find the quiet she frequently craved.

Where would she go for comfort after she moved to Northumberland? Would there even be a place to run to? Would she need to? What kind of husband might Bost be?

She tried to push the thoughts from her head and focus on nothing more than the leaves rustling overhead, but she couldn't shake her worries.

It was perhaps not fair to Bost that she was already contemplating moments of escape. For all she knew, he would be an exemplary husband. She might be the shrew from which *he* yearned for freedom. The only thing she knew for certain about marriage was that the best ones were a partnership.

The problem wasn't Bost, she realized. It was

that she did not know him. They had not chosen each other. He didn't know the first thing about her. Nor care to. She clenched her fists at the infuriating sensation of being immaterial to her own future. She and Mr. Bost had no relationship whatsoever. She'd had a deeper heart-to-heart with Lord X at the masquerade than she'd ever had with her future husband.

Add to that the thought of living so far away... Even if Mr. Bost turned out to be a perfectly wonderful man—a "firm, but doting" husband, her mother might say—a life so far from London, so far from her family, from the familiar comfort of her favorite river, of familiar sights and sounds and smells... It would be too miserable to bear.

So she wouldn't think about that. Not until the wedding was over and she was being handed into the carriage.

For now, she would concentrate on what she could look forward to. A lazy afternoon counting leaves. A carriage ride with her sister. An assignation with the mysterious Lord X at Lambley's next masquerade ball. She couldn't help but grin.

Contrary to Camellia's earlier assumption, Bryony had not at all been put out to discover her sister's entrée to the masquerade had been a shocking success. In fact, Bryony had taken the money their mother had earmarked for her youngest daughter's gown at Camellia's wedding and spent it on an entirely different sort of ensemble instead. Bryony had given it to Camellia to wear at the next masquerade.

The jewel-toned gown was a deep ruby hue, with a whispery silk skirt and bodice lined with glass stones that would sparkle beneath the candlelight. She could scarcely wait to witness Lord X's reaction. Smiling at thoughts of what he might say, she drowsed to the sound of the water, her mind at peaceful harmony with nature.

All too soon, however, her two hours were nearly up, and Camellia had to make haste in order to meet her sister at the appointed time. She eased up from her prone position and rolled her shoulders to loosen the muscles. She couldn't stay in her hideaway forever. Dahlia was counting on her.

With a resigned sigh, Camellia slid down from the rock and brushed the dirt from her pelisse as best she could. She was running out of time. Her mother wouldn't be at the door to notice and the maids were long used to Camellia's mysterious dirt stains, so she did the best she could and then hurried across the grass to a spot where a break in the trees rejoined an old path through the park.

She leapt across a fallen log and onto the old trail—only to take a header straight into the fluffed cravat of a gentleman out for an afternoon stroll.

"I'm so sorry," she gasped. "I was running because… there might have been a… squirrel?"

The lie died in her throat as she belatedly recognized the gentleman she'd barreled headfirst into.

"Miss... Grenville?" Lord Wainwright stared at her in understandable confusion, then smiled as if her crashing into his sternum had been the highlight of his day. "Why, of course you are. Do help me out—I am dreadful with names. Are you the one who performs at musicales or the chit with the champion whinny?"

"All Grenville girls have whinnies as strong as their fine teeth," she answered with a straight face —until she realized she'd just done the unthinkable. She'd exchanged jests with the enemy. The despicable Lord Wainwright.

Alone.

In the woods.

Miles from anyone.

"What are you doing out here?" she stammered, clutching her pelisse tighter about her bosom.

"I've just slipped my duenna," he replied with a pointed look over her shoulder at the distinct lack of chaperonage joining them on the trail. "I don't suppose you could loan me yours?"

"She's got the ague," Camellia replied quickly. "It may be catching. I do hope I haven't passed it along to you. I haven't any quicksilver handy."

"*Females.*" The earl gave an exaggerated sigh. "Why does the fairer sex insist upon carrying reticules and then fail to stock them with anything useful?"

Camellia glared back at him. She hoped. She definitely did not want him to believe she found him charming. Or that their ridiculous conversation reminded her of the teasing volley of insults she had been known to exchange with her brother and his friends. She bit her lip.

Of all the conversations she might have had with a wicked, rakish earl in the middle of the forest with no one about... the last thing she'd expected him to do was put her at ease.

Well. She would not do the same. If he chose to waste his money on courtesans and cravats, that was his own business. But Lord Wainwright was the enemy of her sister and behaved far from honorably with the wives of his friends. She could not forgive him. There was nothing Camellia valued more than friendship and family.

"If you'll excuse me," she said briskly. "I am very busy. The vicar is joining us for supper. He'll be giving a lovely talk based on my favorite Bible verse on the evils of fornicators, and I do not want to miss it."

Lord Wainwright blinked as if nonplused.

There. She tried not to feel smug. That wouldn't put him in his place—she doubted anything could—but at least she'd established herself as pious and her family as God-fearing. If that didn't scare him away, nothing would.

"Your favorite Bible verse," he repeated slowly. "About fornicators. Which passage did you say?"

Blast the man. The only verse she knew for certain was the passage about adultery in the reading of the Commandments. She gritted her teeth. Why hadn't she thought to condemn adultery instead of all fornication? Nothing for it. She was going to have to invent a Bible verse.

"Genesis," she said with as haughty a tone as she could muster. "Chapter fifteen."

"All of it?" he asked politely.

She gritted her teeth. Splendid. Now she either had to carry off a convincing lie... or look like a madwoman.

"Verse nine, of course." She lifted her nose and assumed an authoritative manner. "'For lowly is he who lies with the wife of his neighbor, and shall burn in hell for the lies he hath told and the pain he hath wrought upon others.'"

There. That sounded... possible. She hoped.

With an assent of his head, Lord Wainwright stepped back and motioned her to continue on her way.

She kept her head high as she stalked around him and headed down the path to the main trail. But she couldn't stop a smile from curving her lips at having hoodwinked him so easily.

Of course a licentious rakehell had not recognized an invented quotation. With luck, she'd even given him food for thought regarding his unforgivable conduct slaking his lust with the wives of his friends. And even if all she'd accomplished was causing him to think her a demented old bird... Then good. He'd leave the Grenvilles alone.

She couldn't wish for anything more.

CHAPTER 7

*M*ichael peered over the edge of the balcony at the teeming crush of masked merrymakers below. He had promised himself he wouldn't look—he'd been craning his neck five times a minute even when no new guests had been announced—but he could not stop himself from peeking just one more time. And perhaps another.

He couldn't wait to see Lady X. Had been looking forward to their encounter ceaselessly since the moment she'd disappeared from his arms seven days earlier. All week long, his heart had quickened every time he caught a glimpse of blue from the corner of his eye.

"Lady X!" the doorkeeper called out below.

Eagerly, Michael's gaze flew back to the entrance. A willowy blonde strolled in wearing a peacock-feathered mask and a come-hither smile. His shoulders sagged. Not his Lady X. He would have to keep waiting.

The past sennight had been far more trying than he'd anticipated. Keeping out of the scandal columns meant a complete reversal to his routine. He'd avoided the theater, Vauxhall Gardens, his friends, his gentlemen's clubs, gaming parlors, gatherings of any kind where the least noteworthy person, conversation, or scandal was likely to occur.

Michael had even had to limit his interactions with guests at his *own* party, lest he be accused of flirtation or debauchery. He would have canceled the bloody soirée altogether, were the cancelation itself not just as likely to land his name in the papers, along with salacious conjecture about what activities a famed rake might be pursuing instead of honoring his invitations to his guests.

"Lord and Lady X!" came the next cry.

Michael couldn't prevent himself from looking, even though he knew it would not be her. If his Lady X had accepted his invitation, she would arrive alone rather than with a lover. And yet here he was, gripping the banister with nervous excitement in the hopes that it *was* her, just to put him out of his misery.

It was not.

He slumped back against the wall. Soon. She would be here soon. If he could survive the past week, he could survive another hour or two.

Although Michael had never been the sort of person who sat about his house doing nothing, he had spent a week trying to do exactly that in order to keep his name out of the papers. Forty days without scandal. Thirty left to go. His shoulders tightened.

It had sounded so easy. Not anymore.

He *had* to win this wager. Not for the money. To prove himself to his friends. He needed someone to believe he was more than a walking caricature. He needed this to be a new beginning.

"Lord X!" came the next cry.

Michael looked. He couldn't stop himself. Even though the chances of Lady X arriving at the masquerade dressed as a man were preposterous enough as to be impossible—God help him, he looked.

Not Lady X. Definitely a man.

With a groan, he leaned his head back against the wall and tried to be sensible. He'd been trying all week. When staying inside had proved too maddening to endure, he had made a list of the most innocuous, scandal-free destinations London had to offer, and visited every last one of them. The haberdasher. The linen maker. The button shop.

When he'd run out of ideas, he'd taken to the park rather than go back home to his overlarge, empty house. He didn't visit Hyde Park to race a curricle down Rotten Row or promenade in his stately coach with the family crest. Those were activities where he was liable to accidentally make eye contact with the wrong person and end up caricatured for weeks.

Instead, he'd tied his horse at an unused post in the least attended sector, and hiked off down the most solitary trail he could find. Surely scandal would not find him in the middle of the woods.

Except it almost had. He'd run into the eldest Grenville—literally, as it would happen—and the daft chit wasn't even accompanied by a chaperone. If they weren't in the most remote thicket of the park's endless acres, someone might have chanced upon them alone together. The chit would be ruined, Michael would be leg-shackled, and the caricatures that would follow...

He shuddered. *That* had been a close call. And a good lesson. He would not be returning to that park until after the bloody wager was over. In fact, he ought to strike "solitary walks" off the list altogether. The last thing he needed was an accidental compromise.

"Lady X!" called the doorkeeper.

Michael's head swung out over the balustrade like a lapdog from a carriage window.

No sapphire blue.

The beautiful, dark-haired woman who eased into the crowded chamber wore a raven feather mask and a stunning blood-red gown with stones that sparkled like diamonds along the neck of the bodice.

As he watched, she reached up and idly worried one of her dewdrop earrings, just as Lady X had the week before, on the balcony behind the painted divider. His blood raced. It was her!

He rushed down the stairs toward the vestibule door, no longer caring if he looked to the others like a green, eager pup. He felt like one. Behind his mask, he didn't give a damn about the judgment of others. All he cared about was Lady X. He just needed to coax her to come with him before some other masked blackguard spirited her away.

In seconds, he was at her side.

"Lady X, I presume?" His heart was still pounding and his breath a bit too quick, but he'd made it. He was the first at her side.

"Lord X." Her red lips smiled up at him from beneath her impenetrable black mask. "It's a pleasure to see you again."

"The pleasure is most definitely mine." He proffered his arm. "Come with me."

"Should I?" she rejoined archly.

"I shall beg if I must."

Only when her fingers curved about his elbow did his tense muscles finally relax.

He guided her up the slender staircase lining the far wall. When they reached the upper promenade, he led her not to the balcony overlooking the back garden, but to a hidden corridor with a second, smaller staircase, twisting up a dark tower.

She tilted her head. "What's up there?"

"Come and find out." He stepped into the darkness, held out his hand, and waited.

She placed her white-gloved fingers in his.

"I've been thinking of you all week," he said roughly. "It's been maddening."

"Why didn't you stop?"

"I can't." He pulled her into his arms and slanted his mouth over hers.

The last time he'd kissed her, he'd felt she was holding back on her passion. He didn't want her to. Not with him. Not tonight. He cradled the side of her face in his hand and told her with every kiss that there was no need for circumspection. No need to be tentative.

Whoever she was before she stepped through the vestibule door, here she was a goddess cloaked in darkness and sheltered by the night. They were as anonymous as stars in the sky, their passion as bright. Her power was boundless. With naught more than the taste of her kiss, she was capable of bringing him to his knees.

Heart pounding, he pulled away while he still could.

Before his baser instinct could tempt him to remain sequestered in a clandestine stairwell for the rest of the night, he locked his hand with hers and drew her up the narrow steps.

"Where are we going?" she asked breathlessly.

Good. She made him breathless, too. He squeezed her hand. "Somewhere we can put our lives into perspective."

When they reached the top landing, he shoved open the thick wooden door to expose the night.

Chill air swept through his hair and swirled behind them. Unfettered stars spilled across an infinite sky. There were no walls, no ceiling, no sounds but the night.

"The roof," she said in wonder, then pulled

from his grasp to race to the edge and peer over the knee-high parapet to the sparkling city below. "It's beautiful."

His heart pounded as he pulled her back from the edge. "*You're* beautiful."

"I'm masked," she said, her voice droll. "You cannot see me."

"But I can hear you," he insisted softly. "You're beautiful inside, no matter how you look beneath the mask."

She lowered her gaze and gestured at the unbroken expanse of wide, smooth stone covering the hundred-odd chambers of the ducal residence. "Now that we are here, what do you intend to do with me?"

Michael crossed to the satchel he'd placed beside the parapet in anticipation of her arrival and opened the flap. Nerves and excitement rushed through his veins. He extracted the two crystal goblets nestled inside a thick woolen blanket, and the bottle of wine he'd been saving for the perfect occasion. He hoped this was it.

With more self-doubt than he'd felt in years, he shook the folds from the blanket, letting it billow out from his chest like sails caught in the wind. A smile tugged at the corner of his mouth. Carefully, he arranged the soft wool over a section of smooth stone in the center of the roof and placed the bottle of wine at one corner.

After he settled the two crystal goblets on either side of the wine, he straightened his shoulders and turned toward Lady X.

The quarter-moon was to her back, casting her face in even more shadow than the black-plumed mask disguising her eyes. If she found his attempt at an anonymous romantic picnic laughable, she refrained from comment. Nor did she make any move to join him.

The back of his neck heated. "Too rustic?"

"Too perfect," she breathed.

Relief flooded him.

Lady X crossed over to the arrangement and stretched out on the blanket until she lay propped on one elbow with her head just below the wine bottle. Her gloved fingers tapped the empty space on the other side.

"Are you going to join me?" Starlight caught her smile.

"Absolutely." He withdrew the corkscrew from the satchel and hurried to her side. "Wine?"

"A little." Her voice was mysterious. "I wouldn't want to do anything reckless."

"I would not dream of it." He poured her a goblet of wine. "You might be hideous behind that mask, remember?"

She laughed and smacked him on the shoulder before accepting the goblet. "Of course I remember. Who says I'm ever unmasked? Perhaps I am the Maiden in the Iron Mask."

"That sounds like an intriguing opera." He raised his glass. "And a performance I would definitely love to see."

"If I ever perform on Drury Lane, you'll be the

first to know." She clinked her goblet with his and smiled up at him after she took a sip. "Delicious."

Pleasure rushed through him. He lay back on the blanket facing the stars, and motioned for her to join him. She placed her goblet aside and laid her head against his arm, careful not to let any other part of her body touch his.

Lady X was by far the most mysterious creature he had ever known.

He pointed at the stars. "Ursa Major. Do you see it?"

She shook her head. "I've never been clever at picking out constellations. I… am not usually out of doors late at night."

"Then I'm glad you're here with me. I love the stars. My father taught me." His heart warmed at the memory. "When I was very young and supposed to be fast asleep, he would sometimes come to the nursery and carry me outside to see the stars."

"That's beautiful," she said with a smile. Then her tone turned dry. "I don't think I spoke with my father until I was out of the nursery."

"It's unseemly," he agreed, not bothering to hide his sarcasm. "Children should be seen and not heard. Ask any respectable family." His father had been criticized for his softness. For giving Michael the moments he treasured most. "But I appreciated it very much. It's one of my favorite memories with him."

"And your mother?" she asked.

"An angel." For years now. He missed her, too. "What about yours?"

She laughed quietly. "Absolutely impossible. Her idea of being the perfect mother is raising the perfect daughter, and ensuring I live exactly the same unobjectionable, predictable, unceasingly proper life she did."

His lips quirked. "I'm sensing... tension?"

"Our family makes Punch and Judy look sane." She nestled her head into the crook of his shoulder. "Mother means well, which makes it even worse. I can't say no. We love each other. So we go on as we always have."

"Should you?" he asked. He would never have dared such a personal question if the masks and the stars didn't make him feel as though he and Lady X were alone in the universe. "Think about it. If you could change any one thing about how you were raised, what would it be?"

"More... control over decisions that affect me," she said at last. "Fewer expectations."

"Too many responsibilities?" he asked with curiosity.

"Sometimes I wonder if I was ever a child," was her cryptic answer. She tilted her feather mask toward the sky. Whether she knew it or not, Ursa Major watched over them both. "What about you? What's the one thing you would change about your childhood?"

"Keep my parents longer," he said without thinking, then immediately regretted the blurted response. He'd meant to keep the topics light. For he and Lady X to have fun together whilst blanketed by midnight. Not to discuss their own darkness.

But it was true. He'd had an idyllic childhood until a fever had struck his parents while they were on a tour of the Continent. He'd begged to go and see them, but his temporary guardian would not take orders from a child. The next day, Michael was no longer a mere twelve-year-old. He was an earl. The first thing he'd done was to ensure he was never powerless again.

"What are your friends like?" he asked to change the subject.

"Even loonier than our mother," she responded, her voice cheery. "My closest friends are my mad siblings."

"Of the Punch and Judy show?" he asked doubtfully. The puppets she'd referenced were quick to fly into tempers.

"The very same. You should see the bruises on my knee from all the love taps my sister gives me."

He brightened. "May I?"

"No." She handed him his forgotten goblet of wine and leaned up on her elbows to drink from hers. "What about you? Do you have close friends?"

"A few." That was an understatement.

Michael had so many friends, so many crowds of acquaintances and swarms of names and faces he vaguely recognized, so many invitations from the second cousin twice removed of the third viscount's nephew's neighbor, that he never sat down and specifically sorted his countless connections into neat piles.

If he had, however, the stack entitled True Friends would contain two names. The first was Gideon, the owner of the Cloven Hoof, currently decorated with yard after yard of strung etchings of Michael's cartoonish misadventures, as conceptualized by London's prolific caricaturists.

The other was Lord Hawkridge, penniless marquess, and the owner of the biggest, purest heart of any man of Michael's acquaintance. Those two unrepentant rotters were the very reason the forty-day wager had sprung to life in the first place.

Anyone else would have gossiped about the caricatures behind Michael's back. The rest of London, in fact, fit neatly into that category. Gideon and Hawkridge were the only ones to throw his overblown reputation in Michael's face. To force him to do something about it. To open his eyes.

Hawkridge and Gideon ribbed him not out of cruelty but because they were friends. No one else would dare disclose their honest opinions about Michael to his face. No one but Hawkridge and Gideon knew him well enough to know that the caricatures were caricatures.

That their well-meaning intervention had resulted in pennants of etchings and a marquess-beggaring wager inscribed in a public betting book, well... Michael chuckled. Perhaps the

Cloven Hoof was more like Lady X's Punch and Judy family than he had realized.

He and Lady X might have far more in common than it already seemed.

"If you could wake up tomorrow with any ability you can imagine," he asked suddenly, "what would it be?"

She was quiet a long moment, then drained her goblet before replying. "You first."

He deserved that, he supposed. His lips curved wryly as he lifted his own goblet to stall for time.

His initial response, the gut emotion that had caused him to blurt the question in the first place, was that he was weary of being infamous. It wasn't that he wished to be respectable in the sense of "staid" or "proper" or "boring." He wished to be respectable as in respected. For his voice to have weight in Parliament, for his presence at soirées and dinner parties to be seen as overtures of friendship, not reconnaissance for his next assignation.

But being seen as something more than the Lord of Pleasure wasn't a special ability. It would be an inversion of his world. Nothing short of a magic wand could reset the closed minds of everyone in London.

"Music," he said instead. It was just as true, and perhaps slightly more possible. "Since the moment you put the thought into my head, I cannot stop wishing I did play an instrument."

"Then you should," she answered simply. "Can you not hire an instructor?"

Not without word of his musical endeavor leaking to the scandal columns. His jaw tightened in frustration. Much as he might like, he would never learn to play the harp. The pianoforte perhaps, a violin if he wished, but the instrument of the angels? He would be a laughingstock. The caricaturists would drown in seas of gold. His lip curled at the thought. No. He would honor his parents' memory, not make a mockery of it.

"What about you?" he asked. "Play fair. I shan't pour more wine until you answer the question. If you could wake up with any quality you don't have today, what would it be?"

"I would be bolder," she said without hesitation. "Even without the mask."

He sat up in surprise. "Bolder in what way? What do you want that you're not going after?"

Her whispered response was almost too soft to hear. "Everything."

CHAPTER 8

*B*reathless, Camellia gazed up into Lord X's fathomless black mask. She could not see his eyes. Even his brow was hidden. There was no way to know what expression he wore. Nothing to go on except the words he spoke. Yet there could be no other answer to his query.

Bolder. She had longed to be bolder, yearned to be someone *else* since the moment she realized it was too late to change her personality. Dahlia was forceful, Bryony was fearless, but Camellia watched from the shadows. Looking out for her sisters. Being a good girl. A proper young lady. Minding every one of high society's interminable rules as if the price for bending them was death. Perhaps the cost of denying her own desires was just as dear.

She was tired of being perfect. The only way to never break a rule, to avoid disappointing anyone's expectations, was to never do anything at all. That wasn't life at all.

Yet who was at fault? If she was nothing more substantial than a music box, nothing but a dutiful automaton respectable enough to possess an Almack's voucher and too terrified to use it, then it was because she had let herself be programmed that way.

She wanted to change. Needed to. Perhaps it wouldn't be for the better, but it would be more authentic—she would be more *herself*—if once in a while she did what *she* wanted, instead of molding to the wishes of everyone around her.

"Bolder," she repeated. "I want to be bolder. It's the one thing about my life I would alter."

"I can grant you that wish." He pushed his goblet away and sprang to his feet. "Be fearless here. Tonight. With me."

He held out his hand.

Simultaneously hopeful and nervous, she placed her fingers in his.

"Whatever it is that you want, you need only be bold enough to ask." He pulled her to him.

Her heart pounded so loudly, she feared he could feel it through his layers of shirt and waistcoat.

"What do you want?" he asked softly. "Be bold. Let me give it to you."

What did she want, here, with him? She closed her eyes and let the night be her guide.

Now that they were no longer nestled on a woolen blanket, the breeze was cool against her bare upper arms... but not overly so. The warmth from Lord X's body heated her whether they were lying prone or standing chest-to-chest beneath the moonlight.

The scent of his breath so close to her lips was as sweet as the wine they had shared. The sounds of the night—if indeed there were any other than the thundering of her heart—were eclipsed by the siren call of the orchestra, whose seductive waltz spilled out through the open doorways and up from the balcony overlooking the garden to kiss their feet, even out here on the roof.

She opened her eyes. There was only one answer. One thing among the many she'd never done that he alone could give her. Without scandal. Tonight.

"I want to waltz," she admitted hesitantly. "But…"

He shook his head. "With me, you never have to justify yourself or your desires. I will never say no."

Her breath caught at his words. "Why?"

"Because I want to be the reason for the sparkles in your eyes." His husky voice was intoxicating. "You want to waltz? We waltz."

He took her hand and turned toward the stairs.

She held her ground.

He looked over his shoulder. Though the expression behind his mask was a mystery, every inch of his posture asked a silent question.

"Here," she said. *Boldly.* "I want to waltz here. Where it's just you and me and the stars."

He stepped forward and took her into his arms without another word.

At first, she thought he might kiss her. Her heart thumped. She was pressed tight against him, her lips tilted up toward the sensual line of his mouth.

And then he took her hand in his and swung her in time to the music.

Her pulse thrilled at his touch. Never had a moment been so magical as dancing across a rooftop in the arms of a dashing stranger. The wind whipped through her hair, tugging tendrils free from her careful chignon, fluttering the ruby silk of her skirt about her legs.

None of that mattered. All she cared about was the hand holding hers. The warmth of his fingers against the small of her back. The strength in his arms, his body, as he whirled her from one stunning night view of London to another.

The night was crisp but his embrace heated her to her core. She could no longer feel her feet flying across the roof to their private rhythm, or the whispery material of her gown fluttering against her silk stockings in the breeze.

All she could feel were her trembling fingers tucked against his warm palm, the strength of his arm tucked about her waist, her lips curving into the widest, most unabashed smile she'd ever experienced.

This was life!

Every part of him was danger and romance

and adventure. He transported her not just from one soaring section of the roof to another, but to an alternate world. One in which she was exactly the woman she pretended to be. Carefree and wild and bubbling with joy at the consuming, heady sensation of being truly, completely, wonderfully alive.

Being in his arms stole her breath, yet gave her strength. He did not look through her as so many men had done throughout her life, but rather as though he could not look anywhere else. As if the sight of her in his embrace was so entrancing, so intoxicating, that he too had forgotten everything and everyone until all that remained was the two of them. Their bodies entwined in a waltz that found its music in their very souls.

Tonight she wouldn't run away at midnight. She would dance in his arms until dawn.

CHAPTER 9

*M*ichael spent the entirety of the following morning with a sappy smile on his face. His especially boisterous mood was entirely due to the aftereffects of spending a few stolen hours with a mysterious, ruby-clad minx.

This time, he hadn't lost her until almost sunup. Nearly twice as much of her company as the last time. His heart felt light. He was ever so grateful the duke had been hosting weekly masquerades rather than fortnightly. Michael never had to go more than seven days without an unforgettable evening with Lady X.

And yet it still wasn't enough.

He stared across the otherwise empty dining table in the center of an equally empty supper room and wished he hadn't taken his habitual late luncheon alone with his thoughts, but had Lady X here to accompany him. He had no idea if she liked pheasant with French sauces, and would have liked the chance to find out.

Not that such a scenario would ever occur. For one, a request to exchange names was expressly forbidden, and Michael had no desire to fall from the Duke of Lambley's good graces.

For two, the ill-begotten forty-day wager was only a quarter through, and nothing would splash his name back into center stage quite like the scandal columns believing the Earl of Wainwright was playing beau.

But the third and most important reason was that Michael loved the mystery. Their encounters were *fun*. He would not wish to spoil it by finding out who she was—being underwhelmed with the truth. He loved the fantasy. Loved not knowing what to expect. Such an opportunity was not something he was often afforded in his real life, and so far the experience was more exciting than he could have hoped.

What would it be like to see her outside of the masquerades?

If Lady X were here, she might surprise him by asking to do some utterly mundane activity in a completely new way. Dance on tabletops. Take tea in a tree. Or she might shock him with more absurdities from her Punch and Judy family. Perhaps her brothers were professional boxers. Perhaps her sisters were fencing masters.

Rather than regale him with tales of her family, Lady X might chastise him for sitting by himself in an empty dining room long after the dishes had been removed, dreaming about things that were not instead of taking action with the things that were.

He *should* play an instrument. His jaw lifted with determination. As a familiar face in the caricatures, Michael had very good reasons for not hiring an instructor to teach him the harp, but those reasons were no excuse at all for why he didn't pick one up and try to figure it out on his own. Why not start now?

Grinning to himself, he quit the dining room and leapt up the stairs two at a time lest he lose confidence in this new plan.

The harp room was at the east end of the main corridor. Because of an obsessive need to protect its contents, the chamber was off limits to guests. Just to be safe, so was the entire east wing of this floor. The opposite wing held the guest quarters. Since none of Michael's guests ever stayed the night, this floor rarely got used at all. It was nothing more than wasted space.

That would change, he decided. He would learn to play, and to do so, he would visit every day if necessary. The harp room would be full of music once more. Steeling himself against the memories, he opened the door and strode inside.

For the first time in many years, its familiar cherubic paintings and rows of collected harps did not fill him with the bittersweet nostalgia he'd battled since his youth.

Perhaps his annual purchase of a new harp for the collection was not him succumbing to the pain of the past, but rather a tribute to what his parents' memories might bring to the future. His heart lightened.

According to family lore, the spacious, sunny music room had once been a heavily trafficked sitting room for one of Michael's great-grandmothers, whose worsening gout no longer allowed her to attend functions. She had combined two smaller rooms into one large chamber in order to let in more sunlight—and more people.

Her daughter was the one who had commissioned the cherubs. She and Michael's grandfather had just returned from a trip to Rome, where the wondrousness of Michelangelo's Sistine Chapel had made a lasting impression. That influence was even how Michael's mother had decided upon his name.

She was the first to bring music into the airy, painted room. Michael had little doubt that his mother's choice of harp as instrument was inspired by her surroundings. The beloved specimens she had once played were old and worn, though the servants were under strict orders to treat each specimen as if it were brand new.

The other harps varied in size and quality. One was a small ivory harp Michael had won over a Faro table at the Cloven Hoof. Others he'd picked up at various music shops during his Grand Tour or later holidays. His journeys to far flung havens of music had become something of an annual pilgrimage. The visit to the music box factory in Switzerland had been a serendipitous perquisite to just such a trip.

His favorite of all the items in his collection was not even a playable instrument. It was a slender, thumb-size harp made of solid gold. His father had commissioned it as a necklace bauble for his wife on the tenth anniversary of their marriage—two short years before their lives were over.

Michael's mother had adored that tiny harp above all things, and had declared her husband had given her a gift of music she could keep with her at all times. His heart warmed. *That* was a woman who would appreciate her son plucking at strings to carry on the tradition.

Smiling, he crossed over to the mirrored glass dome where he kept the golden harp. He froze.

It wasn't there.

He stared blindly, his chest tight with fear. He launched himself about the clean, tidy room, peering behind curtains and flinging chair cushions and all but tearing his hair from his head.

It wasn't there. It wasn't anywhere.

His mother's favorite harp had been stolen.

He tried to control his breathing. Who would do such a thing? Every muscle shook with anger.

Immediately, his mind flashed back to the soirée that polite manners had not allowed him to cancel. What a disaster. After the guests had gone, his butler had informed him of a tussle that had taken place in one of the card rooms on the ground floor.

Apparently, one of the guests had implied to another guest that Michael had sampled his wife's wares, and the man flew into a jealous rage before the footmen could break up the fight.

Michael could not imagine any man in such a condition evading dozens of footmen to sneak up an unused staircase to steal a bauble from an old necklace… but who else could have done so?

His shoulders slumped. Anyone, he realized. Anyone at all.

It wasn't that the public held any specific dislike for him. If anything, the scandal columns only increased his popularity. But with every new caricature, the rumors grew ever greater. Being invited to his residence was an achievement. Being welcomed into private quarters, an honor.

For some, *sneaking* in without Lord Wainwright or his staff being the wiser would be the ultimate victory. Certainly deserving of a trophy.

After all, the harp room was supposed to be one of the infamous rake's many dens of iniquity. If someone wished to prove they'd dared cross its threshold, what better proof than a tiny gold harp that fit so easily in the palm of one's hand?

A tiny gold harp that meant more to Michael than any other possession in his entire earldom.

And now it was gone.

Sadness flooded his veins but could not dispel the rage.

Limbs jerking, he stalked from the music room in the foulest mood he'd experienced in years. It was too late. The harp was gone. Anger was useless. Michael would have to get past it. Or at the very least, distract himself before he threw a punch at a wall.

Heart thudding, he hurried down the stairs, putting as much distance between himself and the music room as possible. He couldn't bear to be within its celestial walls at the moment. Couldn't withstand the accusing stares of painted cherubs.

His throat was thick with grief. He needed to get out of these walls, go somewhere to clear his head. But where? Somewhere with lots of people and plenty of distractions.

Not the Cloven Hoof. Drinking would keep him focused on his frustration rather than let him forget it. Besides, he had the cursed wager to consider. He wasn't going to compound the loss of an irreplaceable memento with the loss of his friends' respect.

Which left what? A respectable gathering, he supposed. He curled his lip in self-deprecation. Did he get invited to respectable gatherings?

There must be something. He crossed to the mantel and flipped impatiently through the tray of cards and invitations on top. The majority were from the type of individual who most certainly would get Michael's name back onto the scandal columns, but... What was this? He scanned the next invitation with interest.

The Grenville soirée was tonight.

Although he had heard the siblings' talent was impressive, he had never been to one of their musicales. Michael had always felt on display in such environments, even if he wasn't anywhere near the stage. For much the same reason, he rarely attended the theater. Far too many opera glasses pointed in his direction.

A single soirée, on the other hand, was casual and fluid. He was not required to arrive at a certain time, sit in an assigned seat amongst starry-eyed debutantes, or stay until the hosts declared it suitable to leave. A casual soirée meant he could mingle if and how he chose, and leave whenever he pleased. The perfect distraction.

His tense shoulders loosened in relief. Quickly, he slid a few similar invitations into his waistcoat pocket. That was what he would do. Repay the calls of those who had attended his rout. The staid, proper sector, anyway. It might be more tedious than his usual fare, but then again… it might not.

Although more than respectable by society's standards, the Grenvilles were unquestionably odd ducks, and to date far more entertaining than Michael would ever have imagined.

Perhaps they were just what he needed to diffuse the fury boiling in his veins at having been robbed by someone he'd trusted in his house. Someone who would never be invited back—if only Michael knew who it was.

His simmering anger and grief had not diminished by the time his coach arrived at the Grenville estate, but he managed to tuck it below the surface and affect a mien a few degrees less surly than he felt inside.

Before the butler could show him from the anteroom to the main parlor, additional guests arrived at the door. While they handed off their hats and coats, Michael wandered over to a quartet of portraits evenly spaced upon the wall.

The visages represented all four of the younger Grenvilles, if he wasn't mistaken. A handsome lot. The painted profiles appeared a few years old, but the faces were easily recognizable. Though he wished the frames held nameplates. He had always been horrid with names.

The lad he recalled from various gentlemen's clubs. His name was... Harold? No. Heathcliff? Michael's jaw tightened in embarrassment at his inability to recall the right name. It would come to him. Maybe. As to the others... He remembered each of them quite distinctly.

Of the three chestnut-haired beauties, the green-eyed eldest was definitely the one he'd run into in the park. The dark-eyed middle chit was the one who had offered to whinny at his soirée. And the blue-eyed youngest was the one who had been kicked in the ankle for referencing the latest caricature. He tilted his head. Perhaps the middle girl was his favorite. He quite approved of that kick to the ankle. That caricature had been repellant.

"Wainwright?" came a disbelieving voice. "What are you doing here? Fishing in a new pond? The Grenville chits aren't your cuppa. The eldest is a mouse, the middle one a harpy, and the youngest... *that* diabolical creature possesses bigger bollocks than a Clydesdale."

Michael's mood dipped from bad to worse. His temples pounded at the effort to still his temper. He ground his jaw as he turned to see who would have made such appallingly disrespectful statements under the family's own roof.

None other than self-important prig Phineas Mapleton.

Splendid. The evening only wanted this.

"I am not here to romance the entire family," Michael bit out through clenched teeth. "I am simply returning a call. It's polite behavior. You might try it."

"When have *you* ever cared about being proper?" Phineas laughed until his eyes watered.

Michael's humor darkened to a dangerous level. He tried not to clench his fists. Phineas was far overdue for a letdown.

The insufferable buffoon slapped him on the shoulder. "A bit less propriety, eh? If you're not careful, you'll put the caricaturists out of business. A tryst with all three would make for a fine cartoon, even if it means sharing one's bed with a mouse and a harpy."

Michael was of a mood to shake the man silly. And torch the caricaturists' entire shops. He turned away before saying something he would regret... and came face-to-face with the dark-eyed middle sister Phineas had just called a harpy.

No woman deserved to hear such garbage. He was going to have to box Phineas's ears after all.

"Please ignore that imbecile." Michael tamped down his nasty mood and did his best to summon a jest to lighten the terrible situation. "Aren't you a Grenville? Shouldn't you be on stage?"

To his surprise, she glared at *him*, not Phineas, as if Michael's mere presence wounded her more deeply than the repugnant gossip's ignorant slurs. "Tonight is a dinner party, not a musicale. Or can't you read your invitation?" Her cupid's bow lips curved into a sneer. "Shouldn't a soulless cretin like you be fleeing a viscountess's balcony or out seducing debutantes three at a time?"

He stepped backward, his jaw dropping in shock. No wonder the chit was known as a harpy. "A soulless cretin like *me*? I suppose a termagant like *you* will never have to worry about being seduced by *anyone*."

The moment the words left his lips, he regretted having allowed her to prick his foul temper—but it was too late to take them back.

The elder sister had walked around the corner just in time to miss the harpy's needling comments, but overhear every single syllable of Michael's incredibly tasteless reply.

"*Out.*" Green eyes flashing with anger, her stiff arm pointed straight toward the door.

"Miss Grenville, I... I don't know what came over me." Horror flooded him as his cheeks flamed in embarrassment. He turned to the middle sister. "I do apolo—"

"Out!" The elder sister's finger shook with anger but did not waver from pointing to the door. "Must we toss you out by the scruff of your neck, like a common mongrel?"

"That will not be necessary." He drew himself up stiffly.

Given the fiery, pious chit had quoted the Old Testament at him just last week, he would not be surprised if she'd rather smite an earl than toss him out on his ear.

He sketched the slowest, most elegant bow of his life, then walked out the door with his head held high.

Until he reached the street.

He could not believe how badly he'd bollocksed the situation. Or that he had been ejected, but Phineas Mapleton had somehow managed to avoid the ladies' wrath—despite instigating the entire debacle.

Michael clenched his fingers in frustration. Bugger paying calls on respectable folk. When he climbed into his carriage, he sent the driver straight to the Cloven Hoof. At this point in his wretched day, he could definitely use a drink. Possibly several.

With luck, he would never run into any Grenville girls ever again.

CHAPTER 10

*S*o furious she could barely speak, Camellia turned from the despicable Lord Wainwright before his arrogant head was even out of the door and guided Dahlia out of the antechamber and up toward the sisters' private sitting room, rather than toward the soirée.

Fortunately, the only individuals to have overheard Wainwright's outrageous insult to her sister had been the butler, Camellia herself, and Phineas Mapleton. The latter was so notorious for unfounded gossip that even if he dared to publicly repeat private slander toward a Grenville, he was highly unlikely to be believed.

Even Camellia couldn't believe it!

Opine as one pleased about the evils of associating with a libertine, she had never overheard the slightest accusation of Lord Wainwright ever treating a woman *poorly*. His flirtatious reputation was exactly the opposite.

The earl was famous for making every woman

believe she was the center of his regard. The caricatures, the scandal columns, the endless swooning—all that came about because of the handsome devil's captivating propensity to being unerringly, exceedingly... *nice*.

The ill-kept secret to all his many conquests was that he didn't even have to try. Ladies positively *vied* for the opportunity to be despoiled by a charming, unapologetic rake with a flirtatious compliment at the ready.

So why on earth would he insult her sister?

Camellia sat Dahlia down in her favorite window seat, rang for a restorative spot of tea, and then planted herself on the floor at her sister's feet. A wrinkled derrière was the least of Camellia's concerns. Something was very not right.

"What happened?" she asked.

Dahlia closed her eyes and let her head fall back against the bay window. "He called me a termagant."

"You are a termagant," Camellia said gently. "But why would he say so? Lord Wainwright supposedly captures the heart of every woman in sight by simply existing in her vicinity. I've never heard of him insulting someone in their own home, least of all a lady."

"I might not have... acted like a lady," Dahlia muttered. She opened one eye. "I might have called him a soulless cretin, accused him of fornicating with virgins and married women at the same time, and implied he had never learned to read."

Camellia stared back at her sister, speechless. The idea was so preposterous, the behavior so outlandish, she could barely believe her ears.

"The earl was a guest in our home," she reminded her sister in disbelief. "He does fornicate with virgins and married women, and he might be a soulless cretin, but he had an invitation and you know he can *read*. He attended Eton and Cambridge before becoming society's favorite rake."

"I was angry," Dahlia muttered. "He destroyed my school and the hope it brought to the lives of dozens of desperate young women, and he does not even realize it."

"Precisely." Camellia held up her palms. "Think about it. How do you expect someone to respond when you explode at them out of nowhere?"

Dahlia's chin jutted upward in anger. "Are you defending that blackguard?"

"I am not defending him. I do not even like him. I'm defending *reason*." Camellia rose from the floor to join her sister in the bay window. "Be more circumspect. You cannot let your anger with him, no matter how justified, put your own reputation at risk."

"Or what? I won't attract any suitors?" Dahlia scoffed. "I'm not certain that's a loss. How well has your good reputation worked out for you?"

Camellia's lips flattened. "You're right. Mine is

not a love match. I don't know a blessed thing about Mr. Bost. But he has never once been in the scandal columns. He is the 'mature, respectable' gentleman Mother promises him to be."

Dahlia wrapped her arms about her knees. "Which makes him bland. And boring."

"The advantage to such bland boringness is that I am confident Mr. Bost will never embarrass me," Camellia pointed out. "After six-and-twenty years of being relentlessly unnoteworthy, to have a man carelessly ruin my reputation would make the sacrifice all for nothing. Father says Mr. Bost is a good man. You deserve a good man, too. I pray it is a love match. But to achieve that, you cannot make a public spectacle of yourself."

"Very well. I shall cease making a public spectacle of myself." Dahlia narrowed her eyes. "But I won't promise not to do as I wish privately."

A vision of Lord X flashed into Camellia's mind and the back of her neck flushed with heat. She coughed into her gloved hand to hide a tinge of guilt. She might not be the best role model at present, but she would not be hypocritical.

"Privately, one may do as one pleases," Camellia managed to croak.

After all, she could scarcely reprimand her sister for behavior she herself had no intention of curtailing until the last possible moment.

Once the marriage contracts were signed, Camellia would be the dutiful bride Mr. Bost expected. The one he had selected, sight unseen. But until then... there were two more masquerades. She intended to spend them in the arms of a man who cared just as passionately about getting to know her as he did about kissing her. They might not have a future... but they still had a fortnight.

The sitting room door swung open with a bang.

"Thank heavens." Camellia leapt up from the window seat. "Our tea has arrived."

She grinned. It was not just the tea.

It was Bryony.

"Why am I making idle conversation with Mother's well-heeled friends instead of up here in a secret soirée with you two?" Bryony took the towering silver tray from the footman and set it on the small mahogany tea table. "Are we celebrating or conspiring?"

"We are definitely not celebrating," Dahlia replied before Camellia could answer. "And Cam won't let me conspire. At least not publicly. So I suppose that leaves... just having tea?"

"Perfect." Bryony poured the first cup. "I brought more cakes than we could possibly eat, but I have faith that we will somehow persevere."

"We always do," Camellia agreed as she filled her plate with scones and clotted cream.

"I have an idea for the next musicale." Bryony leaned forward. "As servants of the establishment, we are required to play the same twelve songs. Wouldn't it be great fun to play them out of order?"

Camellia laughed. "We mustn't. Mother's

ringlets would spring out of balance. You cannot possibly mean to put her through the humiliation of uneven ringlets."

"You are both mad." Dahlia reached for a lemon cake. "Why do you even do the musicales? You could say no if you wanted to stop."

"I don't want to stop," Camellia said with feeling. The opposite. She dreamed of being a professional soprano as famous as Angelica Catelini or Elizabeth Billington. Impossible, of course. She was destined for Northumberland, not the London opera. "I love to sing. I wish the occasions were not limited to family musicales, but since that's the only choice... I'll take it."

Bryony grinned at Dahlia. "You're just sour grapes because you have no musical ability in a family that's otherwise brimming with it."

"Not at all." Dahlia dropped a cube of sugar into her tea. "Cam and Heath may have incomparable voices, and your skill with a violin is incredible, but even if I did possess a talent someone would be willing to hear, I certainly wouldn't wish to do so up on a stage." She pulled a face. "No, thank you. I much prefer to pull strings behind the scenes."

"Which is why you make a lovely headmistress." Bryony's expression was fond.

Over the rim of her teacup, Dahlia returned the indulgent smile. "You would too, you know. I've never known anyone with a finer head for business. The offer is still open, if you would just consider—"

"I have considered," Bryony interrupted softly. "I thank you very much for your kind and oft-extended offer, but I'm afraid my future does not lie in managing a boarding school. How can you handle wrangling so many young girls?"

"They're more interesting than playing the same set of songs, month after month." Dahlia shuddered. "How can you bear so many people looking at you, watching your every move, listening to your every note?"

Bryony shrugged with a mischievous smile. "I've never minded people looking."

"I might have known." Dahlia turned to Camellia. "But what about you?"

"I actually feel anonymous on stage," she admitted. It was what Camellia loved most about the musicales. She could forget everything else, and lose herself in the melodies. Singing was a transcendental kind of freedom.

"Anonymous?" Dahlia repeated in disbelief. "You find performing onstage anonymous?"

"Every time." They were the best moments of Camellia's life. She never wished for the performances to end. "When I sing, nothing exists but me and the music. I love it. Am I tired of Mother's arrangement? Certainly. I would much rather be lead soprano at the opera, with soaring new arias for every season." She smiled wistfully at the thought. "If I could make my living with my voice, I would."

Bryony sighed. "If only Mother and Father

would permit their genteel daughters to 'make a living.'"

Camellia knew it would never happen. "The only reason they haven't disowned Dahlia over her boarding school is because ladies are encouraged to pursue charitable endeavors."

Dahlia rolled her eyes. "Musicales are 'respectable,' but *professional* actresses and opera singers are too often equated with whores." She affected a virtuous tone. "I'm afraid such 'common behavior' would reflect badly on the entire family, Cam, darling."

"As does everything fun," Bryony agreed. "I recommend Cam do it at once."

"Splendid idea." Camellia didn't hide her sarcasm. "The first thing I'll do when we get to Northumberland is request my husband's permission to be mistaken for a whore at the local theater."

Dahlia jerked upright. "You are not in Northumberland yet. And while we're on the topic…"

Camellia set down her teacup in surprise as her middle sister leapt up and dashed from the room without another word. She arched a questioning brow at her youngest sister.

Bryony shrugged. "She's been mysterious lately. I hoped it was a torrid affair with an ostler or a pirate, but I now suspect she's been dipping into Father's opium drawer. Perhaps she's decided to share."

Before Camellia could respond, Dahlia swept

back into the room bearing an exquisite silver gown. Layers of intricate ruched lace, transparent puffed sleeves, and hundreds of strategic glass rhinestones intertwined to make the entire ensemble glitter as if by diamonds.

Camellia's mouth fell open. "Where did you—"

"It's the gown I commissioned for your wedding." Dahlia beamed at her. "Except I won't be wearing it. You are. And definitely not at your wedding. It's for your next masquerade."

Bryony clapped her hands in glee. "I daresay *that* shall catch her mystery suitor's attention."

"He's not my suitor," Camellia stammered. Her cheeks flushed with both embarrassment and excitement. "But I daresay you're right. Lord X won't let me out of his sight."

Bryony grinned. "No one will."

"I've got the perfect earrings to match." Dahlia bounced on her toes. "And a stunning faux-diamond tiara. Everything but glass slippers!"

Camellia laughed. "Who could dance in glass slippers? My satin ones will have to do."

"Try it on," Bryony begged, her hands clutched to her chest in supplication. "You'll look like royalty."

Camellia held the gown to her chest and twirled about the room in anticipation of the next masquerade.

Between now and when she wed, she would strive to live each day to enjoy the fullest extent of her freedom. She was no longer content to stay on her shelf. Not at the masquerade. Not at home. Not at all.

"Look out, London," she announced, straightening her shoulders with determination. "Camellia Grenville is a wallflower no more."

CHAPTER 11

*M*ichael cursed his abominable luck.

After being kicked out of the "mouse's" house three days prior, he crossed paths with her everywhere he went.

Yesterday, she and her mother had entered Gunter's confectioner just as he was walking out, and now she was crossing St. James street not fifty feet ahead with one of her sisters.

The one that didn't hate him. As far as he knew.

He stepped beneath the awning of Hoby's Boot and Shoe to watch from the safety of shadows.

To his eye, the elder Miss Grenville didn't seem mousy at all. Not when she'd quoted scripture to him at the park. Not when she'd threatened to toss him out on his ear. And certainly not as she laughed behind a slender gloved hand, her green eyes sparkling above wind-blushed cheeks. There was nothing forgettable about her.

She was alternately playful and serious, in accordance with whatever conversation she was having with her sister, her animated expressions captivating even from a distance.

Good Lord, he had seriously misjudged her. Or else society had. He frowned as he tried to recall whether he had heard rumors of her mousiness prior to his ill-fated clash with Phineas Mapleton... or if he'd reached his conclusions simply because there had never been any gossip about Miss Grenville at all.

Michael prowled closer, more intrigued than he would like.

The eldest could hold her own with any man. The youngest was precocious on purpose. And the middle sister... well. Every family had its eccentricities. His lips curved. They were quite a family.

He didn't need the Grenvilles in his life by any means. Would scarcely notice their absence from his social queue. Except—he *had* noticed. Was still noticing. Miss Grenville looked more open, more approachable, than she had at any other moment. Perhaps he should take this opportunity to apologize.

Hesitation kept him rooted in the shadows. He shook his head.

No, he needn't apologize. Not to the eldest Grenville, or at least not right now. His first apology, if he was going to mend his character and develop a positive reputation, was due to her termagant sister. Who was blessedly not present.

Michael winced. That was not an apology he wished to do publicly. He was too close to winning his wager. To creating a new name for himself.

In fact, he was still doing his best at not making public scenes at all. Thus far, it was working. A fortnight had passed without his name in the scandal columns. Fourteen blessed days without a caricature of some private moment passed all over town.

This was definitely not the moment for a public chat with the Grenvilles. Even without the middle sister. Besides, the other two were having too splendid an afternoon for him to ruin it by reminding them of a time they were unhappy.

Another day, then.

Even as he made the resolution not to interrupt, a third bonnet joined the others. The delightfully outspoken middle sister. Perhaps the Grenville sisters' perfect afternoon was about to be spoiled.

As he watched, however, the eyes of the eldest and youngest sisters brightened at her approach. The middle sister was far from sour-faced today. She made amusing expressions and gesticulated wildly as she regaled her sisters with a tale apparently so hilarious that it made the youngest chit hiccup with laughter.

Guilt pricked Michael's conscience. He regretted speaking so harshly to the middle sister. No one deserved to be insulted in one's own home. Nor did the chit seem at all prone to a churlish disposition. He frowned. The only person Michael had ever heard refer to her in a negative manner was Phineas Mapleton—who was hardly an unbiased source of factual information.

What if it truly had been Michael who had spoiled the mood? One person's rudeness did not give him permission to respond in kind. *He* knew he'd spoken out of turn because of an incredibly rotten day. But perhaps she had, too. Perhaps their sharp-tongued encounter had simply been the last straw in a long day for both of them.

He straightened his cravat. The young lady deserved an honest apology. And perhaps catching her in a pleasant humor was exactly the right time for both of them.

Before the women could slip out of sight, he stepped out from under the awning and hurried through the bustling street to catch up to them.

The closer he got, the more struck he was by the sisters' similarities and their differences.

From a distance, one might be forgiven for confusing one young lady for the other. They were all dark-haired, curvy creatures of a similar height, with high cheekbones and upturned noses and cupid's bow mouths.

Up close, however, it was impossible to confuse the sisters.

The middle sister was sharp-eyed and dangerously perceptive. Her animated expressions tended toward the ironic, and her quick, subtle movements gave the sense that she was always alert to her surroundings. He couldn't help but wonder the reason for her heightened vigilance.

The youngest sister's eyes held nothing but mischief. Her confidence was almost a swagger, as if she took nothing seriously, least of all herself. But wide-eyed sarcasm and easy laughter made her far too easy to underestimate. He suspected there was more intelligence beneath her bonnet than she liked to let on.

But the green-eyed eldest, on the other hand, was the most mysterious of the three. Somehow, she'd managed to acquire either no particular reputation whatsoever—or that of a perfect little mouse. Yet she sang for strangers and had sprung to defend her sister with the ferocity of a tigress.

Not only that, but what on earth had she been doing unchaperoned in the remotest corner of Hyde Park? Had it been any other woman, he might have suspected an assignation underway, but there had been no other souls around. Not to mention her unorthodox adieu had included a quotation from the Bible. At the time, he had thought her religious beliefs were what kept her in the shadows, but now...

Intrigued, Michael allowed his gaze to linger. He hadn't the least idea what went on inside her head. To his surprise, he wished he did. She wasn't nearly as easy to label as "the mischievous sister" and "the blunt-spoken sister" seemed to be. Perhaps none of them were, and it was folly to even try. He should simply apologize and move on.

Just as he was about to call out to them, a carriage rattled by, cutting off his view for a frustrating moment.

When the wheels had cleared, the sisters were just turning onto Piccadilly. The bonnets of the eldest and the youngest were angled toward each other, rather than the road. But the middle sister's gaze snapped to Michael as if she'd sniffed him on the wind.

The chill in her dark eyes froze him right where he stood.

He debated how best to proceed. Perhaps... now was not the time to apologize after all. He smiled and waved his fingers in a tentative greeting.

She curled her lip in obvious distaste, turned her back without bothering to acknowledge the greeting, and stalked off behind her sisters.

That answered at least one question, he decided wryly. He should definitely find a less public place for his apology.

He glanced over his shoulder to see if anyone had observed him losing a silent duel with a mere slip of a girl. The caricaturists would roast him for weeks. His shoulders relaxed.

No one was watching, save for the Transfiguration figures in the painted glass windows of St. James church.

Once again, his mind returned to the eldest Grenville sister.

What Bible passage had she quoted to him? Genesis, chapter fifteen, verse... nine, was it? He did not pretend to be unaware of his reputation as a rakehell, but she would have no reason to all but accuse him of practicing adultery. He hesitated.

Perhaps there was more context to that passage than he had gathered from all the "pain he hath wrought" and "shall burn in hells" she had so gleefully quoted.

He ducked into the church and made his way up through the twin rows of walled pews to the altar beneath the arched wooden ceiling. Before anyone could note Lord Wainwright's unprecedented interest in scripture, he flipped the Bible's pages to Genesis until he found chapter fifteen, verse nine.

Bring me an heifer of three years old, and a she-goat of three years old, and a ram of three years old, and a turtledove, and a young pigeon.

WHAT? He paused, blinked, then read it again in disbelief.

Heifer.

She-goat.

Young pigeon.

Strangled laughter burst from his throat as he quickly closed the Bible and stepped away from the altar. He had been had, and good. By none other than an alleged green-eyed mouse. Who was obviously nothing at all of the kind. He shook his head in appreciation.

Only one thing was certain.

There was far more to Miss Grenville—and her entire musical family—than met the eye.

CHAPTER 12

The following afternoon, Camellia joined her family at Astley's Royal Amphitheater on Westminster Bridge Road, just south of Charing Cross. Excitement buzzed through her veins as all six of them filed through the entrance. She had never before attended a circus, and was very much looking forward to experiencing the show.

Based on the cheers of a thousand other spectators crowding the two-foot-high circle and hanging over the balconies of the four-story amphitheater, she was far from alone in her excitement. A thrill went through her at the sight of so many people in one place.

The primary circus was to take place in an enormous center ring in front of the orchestra and a huge square curtain. At some point, the billowing black fabric would swish aside to display a fine stage, upon which vignettes would be performed between acts.

The secondary circus was even larger, and would take place in the dozens of spectator boxes encircling the arena. Camellia gazed about in awe. One could easily believe every class and corner of London represented amongst the crowded rows of curved wooden benches.

As a gift to his daughters, Camellia's father had procured seats in one of the few semi-private orchestra boxes on either side of the main stage. Their entire family filled the second of two long benches: Camellia's brother Heath, followed by Father, Mother, Dahlia, Bryony, and herself.

Normally, such up-close seats were reserved for the crème de la crème of society—or, at least, those who could afford the additional cost. Today was no exception.

The row ahead of them contained none other than Lady Pettibone, a formidable matron who ruled the ton with her imperial aura and exacting standards. Her well-to-do nieces Lady Roundtree and Lady Upchurch joined her with twin expressions of genteel disdain for the common rabble overflowing the cheaper sections. Camellia could only imagine what such esteemed individuals thought of a mere baron and his family.

To the left of the three society ladies sat a trio of well-dressed gentlemen. First, next to Lady Roundtree, was Phineas Mapleton. Beside Mapleton was the handsome marquess Lord Hawkridge. On the other side, seated directly in front of Camellia... sat the distracting Lord Wainwright.

Heaven save her. She tried not to watch him, but he was impossible to ignore.

Even as the orchestra began to play a rousing opening number, her gaze was not on the talented flautists and energetic violinists but rather drawn inexorably to wide, masculine shoulders encased in an indigo tailcoat that looked soft enough to touch.

Not that Camellia would dare reach for him. In fact, it was fortuitous indeed that it was she and not Dahlia who sat behind him, or the earl might have found himself shoved unceremoniously from his exalted bench to the sawdust floor.

Fortuitous seating arrangements for Lord Wainwright, that was. For Camellia, it was torture.

She meant to watch the tragedians and comedians, the riding-masters standing on horseback, the contortionists—really she did. But it was difficult to focus on crackling whips and clowns diving through hoops when the attention of every woman in the crowd was directed right at the handsome earl mere inches in front of Camellia.

Her muscles tightened. She hoped the women hanging over the balconies opposite took care not to swoon, lest they tumble onto the horse-fouled sawdust below. Her gaze returned to the handsome earl whose spotless tailcoat was so close to her knees.

What must Lord Hawkridge think of playing second fiddle to Lord Wainwright's conspicuous popularity? She frowned in thought. The marquess was on the hunt for a fortune... or, at least, a fine-blooded heiress. Perhaps he hoped some portion of the attention the earl attracted would reflect back onto himself.

As for Phineas Mapleton, Camellia suspected the self-important gossip had yet to realize that he wasn't the gentleman all the ladies were cooing at. Mapleton believed his ability to afford Brummell's tailor elevated him to the same echelon of acclaim and respect, when in fact all it did was emphasize the difference.

If it were up to her, the man would never receive an invitation to her family musicales again.

She tilted her head at the mismatched front row in consideration. Did Lord Wainwright always gad about with souls considered lesser catches, or was this afternoon's company merely a coincidence?

Perhaps the fawning ladies were right, and the earl did not distinguish by class or standing due to a kindhearted nature. Or perhaps the envious men were right, and the unrepentant rake carefully arranged his backdrops to make himself look even better.

Whatever the motive, it was certainly working. No feat by the horsemen caused more palpitations of the heart, no daredevil tumble by any clown caused more smiles than Lord Wainwright had by merely gracing the amphitheater with his presence.

She wished she could see his expression. Not because of any desire to gaze upon an outrageously handsome face, of course, but to gauge what the man himself might be thinking.

Was his focus upon the droll comedians and dramatic tragedians? Or did the earl content himself with batting his sinfully long lashes at his legion of rosy-cheeked admirers? Was he thinking something else entirely?

By the time the curtain fell for intermission, Camellia was so irritated at her inability to watch anything besides Wainwright's muscled shoulders that she was half-tempted to request a second curtain be raised between his bench and hers.

Determined not to become engaged in conversation with anyone in the first row, she turned toward her sisters.

"What do you think?" she asked brightly. "Have you ever seen such a show?"

Dahlia's eyes shone. "It was marvelous! I'm thinking of bringing my girls next week. They deserve a bit of fun."

Camellia lifted her brows in surprise. "Can the school afford tickets? Even penny seats become expensive when adding hack fare and all the other little costs."

Her sister's cheeks flushed. "As it happens, I've received an anonymous donation that will keep us afloat for another month at least."

"Why, Dahlia, that's splendid!" Camellia leaned back, as much filled with relief as pride for her sister's ability as headmistress. "How did that come about?"

"Anonymously." Dahlia cleared her throat and

turned back toward their mother before any additional questions could be asked.

Camellia and Bryony exchanged thoughtful glances.

Bryony lifted a shoulder. "I told you she's been mysterious lately. There is no chance the donation is anonymous. I'm still hoping she's become mistress to a rich but rugged ostler or perhaps a dashing pirate."

Camellia shook her head. "Why would there be a pirate in the middle of London?"

"Ostler, then." Bryony tilted her head toward the center ring. "Now that I've seen what a riding-master can do on horseback, I've no doubt a young, handsome one could steal a lady's heart."

"I should hope the three of us aren't so silly that our heads could be turned by nothing more substantial than a pretty face," Camellia said lightly.

At least, she hoped her sisters were the strong ones.

"What else is there?" Bryony's blue eyes sparkled. "There's one in particular I fancy, although I'm sure Mother wouldn't thank me for the scandal."

Camellia couldn't keep her gaze from flicking toward the rakish earl. "Please don't tell me it's…"

"Oh, heavens no. Dahlia would disown me for exchanging glances with that man, much less stolen kisses. Besides, the scoundrel I have in mind is…" Bryony gave an exaggerated shiver of pleasure. "My secret."

"Stuff and nonsense," Camellia chastised her. "You cannot tell me you would dare keep such a secret from your elder sis—"

The curtain flew open and the second half of the circus began.

Probably.

Camellia couldn't quite determine what delights were unfolding in the center ring, because once again her damnable eyes would not quit their focus on the earl in front of her. He had just turned toward his companion, and in the brief moment in which she caught his profile, the earl had smiled.

Her breath caught.

Even though that slow, breathtaking smile had been aimed at the marquess at his side and not the row of Grenvilles behind him, she had felt its impact from her stockings to her bodice.

Little wonder the man got away with murder. No one could possibly keep a single thought in her head when faced with that knowing, devastating smile and those gorgeous hazel eyes.

She distrusted him even more by the second.

And yet, curse him, she couldn't make herself look away.

By the time the final curtain closed, she was all but ready to flee from the amphitheater back into the safety of their carriage. Courtesy and simple logistics, however, dictated that she file sedately behind her sisters as they followed their parents toward the door of the private orchestra box.

Just as it was finally Camellia's turn to exit, a passing groom tripped over a fallen broom. A bucket of muddy mop water in his hands flew from his arms. Its contents slopped to the ground in a growing puddle of rancid goo right at the box exit. Camellia and the entirety of the first row were now trapped inside until the mess could be cleared.

Face flaming with embarrassment, the groom bowed to her and snatched the now-empty bucket from the lake of off-color liquid. "I'm so sorry, miss. A thousand apologies. I'll clean this right up and have you on your way lickety-click, you'll see. It won't be but a moment."

He dashed away before she could answer, presumably in search of tools with which to mop up the spill.

Several feet ahead, Camellia's family had paused to wait. They paid little attention to the temporary delay, and instead seemed locked in some sort of debate involving emphatic gesticulation on the part of her father and brother, interposed with nervous handwringing by her mother.

Which left Camellia to fend for herself against the three most influential society matrons, the single most judgmental gossip of the ton, a handsome marquess, and the rakish, arrogant earl she couldn't get out of her mind.

Full of trepidation, she turned to face the remaining members of the private box.

"Miss Grenville?" gasped Lady Upchurch in disbelief. "How did I miss that you were right behind us? You have the loveliest singing voice of anyone I have ever heard."

"You might have missed her because Miss Grenville very politely wasn't singing during the circus," Lady Roundtree pointed out.

Camellia smiled weakly. On stage, she knew just what to do. Off stage, there was no script to follow. No curtain to end the scene.

"More's the pity. Your singing voice is second to none." Lord Hawkridge touched his hat. "Miss Grenville, you truly are far better than the current reigning soprano."

Lord Wainwright's brows lifted appraisingly. "In that case, she would be an international phenomenon at the opera."

Camellia's teeth gritted at the earl's choice to speak *about* her, rather than *to* her, despite standing less than an arm's width away.

"Miss Grenville? Part of the opera?" Lady Upchurch recoiled in horror. "Obviously she mustn't join the *theater*, Wainwright. Think of her reputation! Why, we'd never be able to associate with a Grenville again."

Indeed. Camellia bared her teeth in a false smile.

The earl had managed to link her name and, by extension, her entire family to the possibility of reputation-ruining scandal right in front of two of society's most uppity busybodies as well as the grand dame colloquially known as the "old dragon" due to her ability to destroy the standing of society hopefuls in the space of a single breath.

"I shan't be singing anywhere but my family musicales," she assured the ladies before the subject could spiral too far out of control.

Lady Roundtree harrumphed. "I should hope not, child. The very thought of you sinking to the level of a common *actress*..."

Mortified that the image had even been put into their heads, Camellia's neck heated uncomfortably. She clenched her fists and sent Lord Wainwright a scathing glare. If she became fodder for salacious rumors... Her skin went cold.

Living through the scandal would be bad enough if she really were an opera singer. But she wasn't. She was no one. On purpose.

In fact, she'd dedicated six-and-twenty years of her life just to avoid embarrassing moments like these. Unobtrusiveness was the perk of being a wallflower. Decades of hiding from the public eye kept her—and her reputation—safe. Yet all it took was one trip to the circus for a single comment from Lord Wainwright to undo all that sacrifice and thrust her straight into the mouth of the dragon.

The next time any of these ladies attended a Grenville musicale, they would think of this moment and recall their threat to give Camellia's entire family the cut direct if she were to be foolish enough to follow her dreams.

She raised her brows at the earl in irritation. He'd started this nonsense. Surely he would come to her aid.

"I don't know," Lord Wainwright said blandly. "I rather like actresses."

Her mouth fell open in disbelief. So much for rescue. Of *course* the cad liked actresses. The profession was often synonymous with prostitution. And now he'd linked her name to the same image.

Lady Pettibone stared down her nose in utter distaste, as if no longer picturing Camellia merely a too-scandalous-to-associate-with opera singer, but now a painted trollop with loose morals. The sort who would be happy to entertain a man like Lord Wainwright however he pleased.

Camellia's face flushed in humiliation.

"Perhaps a moneyed, titled 'gentleman' doesn't mind being the center of scandal, but I have never wished for such attention, and I thank you to cease forcing it upon me," she hissed between clenched teeth.

He raised his brows. "I merely enquire why a woman's talents should be seen as a strike against her."

"It depends on the 'talents,'" Lady Pettibone said coldly, having clearly decided the earl's comments had gone too far. "A lady of good breeding would never give a fallen woman so much as the time of day."

Mapleton dug his elbow into the earl's side with a lewd look. "Wainwright will give anyone the time of *night*, though, eh?" He wiggled his brows. "Perhaps an opera singer is just what the earl needs."

Lady Pettibone's haughty gaze did not waver.

"Opera singers may be suitable for dalliances, but they are *far* from countess quality. Even for a rakehell earl."

"Oh, you mean the Grenville chit?" Mapleton snorted with laughter. "Obviously not her. A mouse that timid isn't countess quality *or* courtesan quality. Too easy to forget in the morning."

Camellia's mouth fell open at the horrific slight. Her cheeks burned. She wanted to sink right through the sawdust. Or beat the earl's pretty head with one of the clowns' wooden sticks. He was unbelievable. First he had made her an object of speculation, then he stood idly by as his associate made her an object of ridicule. She glared at him. Both men were despicable.

"A mouse, am I?" she demanded, her voice shaking with anger and humiliation. She spun toward Mapleton. "You are an insufferable gossip who spreads tales about other people because you've nothing interesting of your own to say." She turned back to Wainwright. "And even a lioness wouldn't want to be this blackguard's countess. You're a successful rake because 'tis *only* women of loose morals who will have you."

Mapleton's jaw dropped open. After a moment of stunned silence, he roared with delighted laughter. "Not even a lioness! Just wait until the caricaturists hear of *this*."

Lady Pettibone rapped the unrepentant gossip with her parasol. "If a single word of this entirely inappropriate conversation gets printed in any scandal columns or scratched into an etching, I will disavow its contents, deny my presence, and ensure you never step foot back into London again. Are we clear?"

Mapleton's laughing countenance drained of color. He swallowed visibly. "Fine. You're hurting Wainwright, not me. He basks in the attention."

"Of course he does," Camellia muttered. What else could one expect from a rake without a heart?

"The last thing I want is scandal," Lord Wainwright assured her, his gray-brown-green eyes wide with innocence.

Mapleton nearly choked in disbelief. "That's only because you've a wager in the betting books claiming you can exist forty days without your name in the scandal columns. We all know *that's* going to fail."

What an absurd wager. Camellia turned away in disgust. The earl was the opposite of men like respectable, mature Mr. Bost. Lord Wainwright was scandal incarnate. His exploits had graced scandal columns and penny caricatures for years. She should not have expected more from him.

Mapleton was right. There was no chance of a rakehell like Wainwright curbing his acclaimed flirtations. The only miracle was that he hadn't lost the bet already.

Camellia stood as far from them both as possible. As someone who had spent her entire life keeping her name out of the gossip columns, she found it appallingly distasteful for a man to be unable to do the same for forty short days.

"Ladies? Gentlemen?" a groom called hesitantly. "The aisle is clear now, if you'd like to exit the box."

Like to? There wasn't anything Camellia wanted more.

She curtseyed to the three ladies, ignored all three "gentlemen," and hastened out of the orchestra box before her once spotless reputation could come to any permanent harm.

$\mathcal{B}$y the time of the masquerade that evening, Camellia was desperate to escape into the night for a few blissful hours in the company of Lord X. She could do well with a restorative dose of anonymity in the arms of a gentleman who had never once let her down. Her spirits lightened.

Lord X would be the last person to allow her to be belittled or permit her to be uncomfortable in any way. From the moment they had met, he'd rescued her from unwanted attention and compounded his chivalrousness by giving her full control over the direction and pace of their relationship.

Her heart tripped. *Relationship.* She could scarcely deny they shared one, no matter how difficult it might be to define. He was why she was here, decked head to toe in shimmering silver, save for a white-feathered mask and gray satin dancing slippers.

More than that, he was the reason she awoke with a smile in the mornings and tumbled into her dreams with a wistful sigh every night. Lord X was open. Honest. Dangerously perfect.

And after tonight, there would only be one masquerade left before she was betrothed to a stranger.

She shoved the disheartening thought away as the doorkeeper pushed open the entrance to the main hall and called out her name. "Please welcome Lady X!"

"Lady X!" the boisterous crowd roared back, glasses of champagne raised high.

A wide grin curved her lips at being back in the mad, exhilarating world of the masquerade. She touched her fingers to one of her earrings as she scanned the upper promenade for the only merrymaker who mattered.

"Lady X," came a familiar husky voice into her ear. "My heart thumps every time your name is announced, but it only leaps when I see that it's you."

Her skin flushed with pleasure as he lifted her gloved hand to his lips.

"Lord X," she murmured. "I wondered if you would be here yet."

"You needn't wonder." He lifted her palm to his cheek before releasing her hand. "I have been wretched with wanting to see you again for an entire week. You have made me a desperate man. It is quite unbecoming."

"You could never be unbecoming," she said, and meant it.

With a crooked smile, he pointed at his mask . "How do you know? I could be alarmingly monstrous beneath the black feathers."

"It would be a very becoming sort of monstrous," she assured him. "The sort that might turn you into a prince, if the right woman were to kiss you."

"Then a prince I must be," he replied softly. "For you have already kissed me."

Camellia's mask hid her blush. She hoped. "I might be tempted to do so again, if you would be so kind as to take me for a stroll through the rear garden. Ever since I glimpsed the stone folly from the balcony, I have been eager to find the path that leads to it."

He brushed the side of her cheek with his knuckles, then proffered his arm. "As you wish."

"Thank you." A sense of contentment washed over her. She looped her arm through his.

"You're very welcome." He touched her hand. "Pleasing you pleases me, my lady."

As before, the sea of revelers parted as if by magic as Lord X led her toward the rear doors on the far side of the chamber. In minutes, they were out of the hot, riotous crowd and stepping into the cool stillness of the night.

Although there were many other couples on the lawn, on the balcony overhead, or on one of the many stone paths below, their low conversations—if indeed there were any—were indistinguishable to the ear. By gazing at Lord X instead of their surroundings, Camellia could almost imagine them alone in the garden with only the stars as chaperones.

"Tell me more about how 'wretched' you were to see me," she teased as they strolled down a winding, circuitous path.

"Wretched is too kind a word for the pitiful creature I have been." He pressed her fingers to his lips in a kiss. "Last night, instead of sleeping, I spent the hours imagining this night instead. How you would look. What I would say. Whether you might press yourself against me in the stairwell again and abuse my poor tender heart with glimpses of passion."

"You're certain it wasn't *you* who pressed against *me?*" she asked.

"It's hazy," he admitted. "Sometimes I get mixed up between what really happened, and the alternative versions that transpire in my dreams."

Amused, she cast him a speculative gaze. "Did you really lie awake practicing what you would say to me tonight?"

"Absolutely. Then forgot every word of it the moment I saw you," he answered cheerfully. "I'm afraid you get the real me, rather than the practiced me. What about you? Have you never rehearsed what you planned to say?"

"No," she replied honestly. When one did not leave one's quarters except to sing memorized songs at the occasional musicales, there were no conversations that needed to be rehearsed.

He glanced at her in surprise. "Not even for tonight?"

"Especially not tonight." She gave him a shy smile and hoped he could see her sincerity. "I want every moment with you to be as deliciously surprising as the last."

"Hmm." He swung her into his arms and raced up a hidden trio of steps that opened into the rear of the stone folly. "Were you expecting that?"

"No," she admitted breathlessly as he set her back on her feet.

"Good." He cradled the back of her head in his hand and lowered his mouth to hers.

Pleasure rushed through her. Not only from his kiss, but from everything about him. The romance of his words. His strength. His passion.

The warmth of his embrace might weaken her knees, but his fearless honesty and eagerness to see *her* captured her heart. His face might be masked, but he willingly bared his soul to her. She had never felt closer to another person. Never imagined it could be like this. Never wanted it to stop. She was helpless to resist.

She wrapped her arms about his neck and opened herself to him. The stars, the night, the *moment* was theirs. She kissed him with six-and-twenty years of loneliness. She kissed him with all the pent up yearning she suffered between each of their far too brief masked encounters. But most of all, she kissed him with the same honesty he'd given to her.

Her pulse quickened as their kisses became

deeper. She wanted him to *know* how interminable each hour was outside of his arms. The highlight of each week was being here, with him. She had missed him far more than was wise, but she was no longer wholly in charge of her heart.

An important piece of it now belonged to him.

When at last they broke their kiss, he led her to a small stone bench between two fluted pillars. They sat in the center, their bodies touching, his warm arm wrapped snug about her to cradle her close.

Only then did she recall that the folly was visible from the balcony. Anyone at all could have seen him swing her into his arms. A dozen revelers might have witnessed their kiss.

Her breath caught. Not with embarrassment, but with excitement. The idea pleased her far more than it should. Despite the royal gown and the extravagant mask, Camellia was a proper young lady. An unremarkable wallflower.

Yet, knowing that no one would ever know it was she who allowed herself to be carried in a stranger's arms, she who returned his passionate kisses on the roof, in the stairwell, inside a folly—the anonymity gave her a power she had never before experienced.

Even Lord X did not know the identity of the woman he was wooing. It was a different sort of attachment. A romance that was only real during the night. As ethereal as a dream.

This was her dream made true. An impossible adventure. Limitless freedom, if only for the night. If others wished to watch, then let them watch. She was not here for them. She was here for herself.

And for Lord X.

She laid her head against his chest and listened to the comforting rhythm of his heart.

"What are you thinking?" he asked.

"For you, what would constitute a perfect day?" she countered, rather than admit the truth.

"This," he responded without hesitation.

"This is a perfect night," she corrected, despite the rush of pleasure at his answer. "What do you do when you can do anything you want?"

He was silent a long time before responding.

"I'm not sure I ever have days where I do solely what I want," he admitted at last. "To some people, it may look as though that's all I do, but the truth is that even when I am not devoting my time to my responsibilities, every action I take, every word I say is often picked apart or misinterpreted or exaggerated beyond its intended meaning. So even when I am doing *what* I want, I am not able to do it *how* I want, which makes it not what I want after all." His self-deprecating chuckle rumbled against her ear. "If that makes any sense."

"I think so." She nodded slowly. "I am rarely misinterpreted, but I live in fear of just such an occurrence. That fear has prevented me from doing almost everything I have ever wished to do."

"Almost everything?" he prompted.

"I'm here," she said simply. "That's more than I would have believed myself capable of even a month or two ago."

"And yet, you must have had a perfect day like you asked me about. Or at least an idea of what yours would be."

"I am lucky enough to have had a perfect moment many, many times," she admitted. Her hideaway restored her equilibrium and gave her peace. "For me, it is a large round rock on the shoulder of my favorite river. No one knows about the spot but me. It is simultaneously open to the universe and completely private. It is the one place I can be free inside my head and out."

"It sounds magnificent." His tone was wistful. "I wish I could see it. I love nature more than anything. Not that I would interrupt your private sanctuary, of course."

"I wish you could," she said softly. "That's what would make it a perfect day."

He wrapped his arms about her and snuggled her closer. "What would we do if we were there?"

"Exactly this." She nestled against him. "Instead of a stone bench, we'd be seated atop the rock, nestled in each other's arms. Instead of a folly, we'd have trees and flowers and a river." She pointed beneath the cupola to the masked couples in the shadows of the balcony. "And instead of merrymakers… we'd have complete privacy."

His lips brushed her hairline. "To do what?"

"This." She cupped his cheek with her gloved hand and brought his head down to meet her lips.

He pulled her close, sinking a hand in her hair as though to keep her locked in his embrace. Foolish man. There was nowhere else she would choose to be. No one else she would rather be kissing. The days that separated them between each masquerade made the nights their mouths joined all the sweeter. Her breasts felt full, her body suddenly demanding.

When she was not in his arms, she yearned for his embrace. Longed for his smile, his scent, his strength, his taste. Here beneath the stars, she belonged only to him.

She parted her lips and allowed him to take possession of her mouth. The rest of her body wished for the same attention. She longed to feel his hands on her bare skin, his mouth anywhere he pleased.

Thank heavens they were in the midst of a lavishly attended masquerade. Had they truly been alone tonight...

She would not have been content with merely a kiss.

CHAPTER 14

*M*ichael wrapped his arms about Lady X and wished life could always be as simple and straightforward as it seemed in that moment. He pressed his lips to her hair.

"This may not completely match your perfect day," he confessed, "but to me it is a close second."

"We said perfect nights don't count," she teased. But something in her voice made him think the only reason she teased was because what they had—whatever it was that they had—was not something they could keep. They were destined to share stolen hours together, not a lifetime.

Nonetheless, within the parameters of their hidden identities, he was determined to respond to her as honestly as he could. He had never been able to be as open with someone as he was with Lady X, and he didn't want to spoil the magic by allowing their connection to become as superficial as all his others.

"Today was the best day I've had all week," he admitted. "And not solely because I finally got to see you, although that would have been more than sufficient."

"Oh?" She tilted her head in question.

"The past several days have been plagued with social encounters that went horribly awry, culminating in the theft from my home of a piece of my mother's jewelry. It is one of the few mementos of her that remain, and to say I was heartbroken at its loss…" Michael grimaced. "Suffice it to say, that was the lowest point of the week."

"What happened today to make it the best?"

"Today, the missing jewelry found its way home." Renewed relief suffused him at his good fortune. "Once I realized the piece was missing, I distributed a drawing of its likeness to every pawnbroker in London. This morning, a messenger invited me to a small shop in Whitechapel, where I was able to buy back my mother's jewelry for far less than it is worth to me." He contorted his face. "There isn't enough money in the world to pay what it's worth."

"That's wonderful," Lady X said, her voice warm. "That it returned home, that is. It's absolutely dreadful that you were robbed. Especially of something with such emotional value."

He couldn't agree more. If he ever caught the contemptible blackguard who had robbed him…

"Perhaps I'm foolish." He forced anger from

his mind and turned the topic back to her. "Have you any trinkets that mean more to you than their monetary worth?"

Lady X shook her head. "I suppose I am the oddity of my family in that way. One of my siblings is a musician, and would die without her instrument. Another has a pet project she values more than her life. The only thing I would hate to lose is something inside of me."

"Your heart?" he guessed. The question came out sounding far more serious than he had intended. Yet he didn't look away. "Here I'd hoped I had a chance of stealing it."

"I am permitting you to borrow it on masquerade nights," she responded primly, then laughed.

Michael did not. The idea that he might possess a piece of her heart, even for only a few hours, had left him light-headed.

"A talent," she said hesitantly. "I have a talent I wish I could use. Were it not unseemly for a lady, I would happily earn a living working every day of the week, if it meant being able to do what I love."

He leaned forward with interest. "What is it you love to do?"

She opened her mouth, then shook her head. "I'm sorry. If I tell you, you might guess who I am."

Might he? Michael straightened with interest. The fact that she considered a successful guess to be possible hinted at some level of notoriety. Intrigued, he ran through a mental list of the most infamous ladies of the ton. Of them, he tried to limit the names to only the ladies with talents capable of earning them a livable wage.

No one came to mind.

He gave up the exercise, frustrated more with himself than over any lack on the part of the ladies.

Every one of them down to a button might boast more talent than he could ever imagine. But since an earl's society conversations were limited to "My, that's an interesting bonnet" and "I believe this is my waltz?" Michael was singularly incapable of knowing whether he and Lady X had ever before met.

Dissatisfaction simmered beneath his contentment. He simultaneously felt that she knew him better than anyone—and that he knew her not at all. Or at least not well enough to satisfy.

He wanted more than stolen moments at a masquerade. He wanted the real Lady X.

His eyes widened in surprise at the depth of his emotion. Perhaps he, too, had been loaning her his heart without even realizing it.

If he knew her identity, they could spend far more time together. Any day of the week, not just when Lambley decided to host a masquerade. They could chat at a dinner party, dance at a soirée, promenade in the park, drop by Gunter's for ices... perhaps even visit the stretch of river she loved so much.

A sliver of hope lifted his spirits. He would

happily dispense with masquerades altogether if it meant more time with Lady X. Indeed, ceasing their double lives would be better for both of them. By attending the masquerades, they both risked the loss of their reputations if their identities were uncovered.

He was surprised to realize the idea worried him far more for Lady X's future than for the outcome of his wager. He still intended to win. He *would* win. He had been a positive saint for almost three weeks, aside from a dust-up here and there with an occasional Grenville.

And, of course, the masquerades.

Everyone who presented themselves at the door was taking a risk. That was a key component of the allure. Yet the true reason Michael had always attended wasn't in order to put a mask on, but rather to take his off. The earl mask, the rake mask, the caricatures of himself. At the masquerades, he was finally just Michael. Even if no one ever knew it.

Until Lady X. She wasn't sitting on a stone folly with a rake or an earl. She was sitting here with him. The real him. And risking her reputation every time she returned for one of their assignations.

Because he'd asked her to risk it, he realized. His shoulders tensed. He'd met her within moments of arriving at her first masquerade. She hadn't intended to come back. He'd begged her. Begged Lambley. Arranged with Fairfax to let her in the door without an invitation.

At the time, he'd thought he was simply arranging to spend more time with an intriguing woman. But that wasn't all he'd asked, was it? His chest tightened. By convincing her to meet like this, he had essentially required her to repeatedly put her reputation at risk. He clenched his jaw. Oh, why hadn't he thought it through?

Perhaps because for him it was different. Yes, his name was often mentioned in scandal columns and his countenance frequently sketched in painfully embarrassing caricatures, but such treatment had little to no impact on his societal standing.

No matter what the rumor, no matter what the drawing, he was still titled. Still rich. Still accepted everywhere.

A woman, on the other hand, was not afforded such luxury. Lady Caroline Lamb had been ruined over scandalous behavior, and she was well-moneyed, well-connected, and wed to an earl. Michael would not be able to protect Lady X if her identity became known.

Granted, a respectable woman attending a masquerade was not as severe a crime as Lady Caroline having an affair with Lord Byron and writing a thinly veiled telltale novel brimming with sordid details. Nonetheless, for Lady X the consequence of discovery would be exactly the same.

Complete social ruin.

Hundreds of otherwise respectable young ladies had lost their reputations over merely being unchaperoned in a room with a man. Much less having repeated rendezvous in private masquerades known for openly encouraging scandalous behavior.

More importantly, he *liked* Lady X. The thought of her suffering any harm, societal or otherwise, was dreadful. Michael wrapped his arms tighter about her.

He didn't want their time together to end. He wanted to get to know the real her. Wanted her to know the real him.

Wished he knew if she felt the same.

While she wasn't looking, he sent her another long, half-infatuated glance. He couldn't tear his gaze from her. Didn't even wish to. Every moment he spent in her company only made him want more. The idea of doing something about it was surprisingly appealing.

Michael had never courted anyone before. Never even considered such a thing. But with her... he would at least like to pay her a proper call. Bring her flowers. See what happened next.

If only he knew her name.

But what could he do? Besides furtive, mooning glances. Whether she answered him or not, the mere act of asking her name broke the duke's strict privacy policies. Michael would be banned for life from all future masquerades.

Gone would be the nights of just being Michael. There would be no respite from the earl mask, the rake mask, the caricatures. Would it be worth the loss?

If Lady X did grant him her name, and permission to see her again, that was no guarantee of a happy ending. She could reject him out of hand once he made his identity known. He swallowed uncomfortably.

Even if that didn't happen, if the relationship turned sour later, he would still never be welcome again at a masquerade. Never able to return to this moment, to this life, to this freedom.

Yet the risk had never been more tempting.

CHAPTER 15

*T*wo days later, Camellia still hadn't managed to put Lord X from her mind even for a moment. She missed their long, candid talks about anything and everything. She missed the warmth of his embrace and the heat of his passionate kisses.

She missed *him*. And she was running out of time.

The future loomed before her, inexorable and empty. There was only one masquerade left before Mr. Bost returned to London to sign the wedding contract and submit their names to the banns. Her mouth went sour with dread.

Three weeks after the banns were read, she would be wed to a stranger. And spend the rest of her life hundreds of miles from home, alienated from her family. From everything and everyone she had ever loved.

Yet it was the right thing to do. For her parents. For her sisters. Even for herself, she supposed.

Despite Camellia's recent attempts to make the most of London's society events while she still had the opportunity to do so, there were no other marriage offers on the horizon, from strangers or otherwise. Her shoulders slumped.

Was it any wonder her mind preferred to focus on the upcoming masquerade, and the last chance she would ever have to spend a few final moments with Lord X?

Anticipation brightened her mood. The new emerald gown she had commissioned in honor of the occasion was nearly ready. Camellia and her sisters had spent the entirety of the previous day scouring shops from Saville Row to Cavendish Square in search of the perfect accessories to accompany the new gown.

All three sisters had pooled their resources to ensure one last magical evening. The perfect mask, the perfect feathers. Bryony had been the one to discover the crowning jewel for Camellia's final night of freedom—delicate teardrop earrings made of intricately cut glass and trimmed with gold.

Now it was merely a matter of surviving the five remaining days until the masquerade—and the five decades of Northumberland isolation to follow. Far from everything she loved.

Rather than wallow in what she could not change, Camellia was determined to keep a smile on her face for as long as she could. For the past two weeks, she had accepted every invitation that crossed the Grenville threshold and intended to keep doing so until it was no longer an option.

She adjusted her bonnet. Today, she and her sisters were en route to Bullock's Museum of Natural Curiosities, where Napoleon Bonaparte's carriage was currently on display. The attraction was already the talk of the town. Camellia would be right in the thick of it.

At the prospect, her body hummed with excitement. She was discovering far too late that she preferred the tumult of the ton to her previous staid existence as a wallflower.

Or perhaps her change of heart was due to the buoyant chaos of the masquerades.

In any case, her brief time intermingling with the ton had thus far been more fun than she would have dared to hope. And ever since her run-in with Lord Wainwright at the circus, she had added a new game to the list: catching the rakehell in scandalous behavior.

She was not a vindictive enough person to go so far as to tattle to the Cloven Hoof in order to ensure the earl lost his ridiculous wager... but she was protective enough of her sisters to take private pleasure when his inevitable failure finally came. Dahlia would survive. The girls who depended on her school might not be so fortunate.

Lord Wainwright needed to learn that his actions had consequences. She lifted her chin. And that not everyone found him as charming as portrayed in the etchings.

To her surprise, however, she had thus far failed to witness the earl doing anything scandalous at all. Instead, she'd caught him admiring flowers at the botanical garden and enjoying a biscuit at Lady Sheffield's tea. Hardly the stuff of social ruin. If one didn't know better, one might believe him to be shockingly... normal. Respectable, in fact.

She did know better, of course. All of society did. As angelic as he might seem during the light of day, the man was infamously devilish by night.

His ridiculous wager would never have come about in the first place had his legendary amorous influence on the heaving bosoms and disappearing purity of impressionable young ladies not been the truth most universally acknowledged in all of London.

When the hackney rolled to a stop in front of Bullock's Museum of Natural Curiosities, Camellia and her sisters alighted from the cab and melded with an impressive queue of sightseers eager to take a peek at Boney's traveling chariot. It had been captured at Waterloo and brought to the Egyptian Hall, where one of its first visitors has been the Prince Regent himself.

Camellia could hardly wait. According to the papers, the spoils encountered inside the carriage's dark blue walls included a gold teapot, a gold coffeepot, gold cups, saucers, sugar basins and candlesticks. All embossed with the Imperial arms and engraved with an ornate N.

"Are you here to see the liquor case, the

writing desk, or the solid gold breakfast plates?" asked a droll voice from just behind her shoulder.

Camellia's heart leapt, then fell. Although she had hoped she recognized the low male voice, it did not belong to the gentleman she wished. It did not belong to a gentleman at all.

"Lord Wainwright," she gritted out in reluctant acknowledgment before returning her attention back to the queue. Six-and-twenty years of politesse prevented her from giving him the cut direct, but no maiden was obliged to be friendly to a rake. Especially not the one who had endangered the future of dozens of schoolgirls.

"I would bow," he said after an extended pause, "but there's little point when you can't even see it."

She sighed and turned around. "Don't you receive enough fawning attention?"

Surprise flicked across his handsome face. "More than enough. I didn't greet you in the hope you would swoon into my cravat. You have the singular distinction of being one of the few who do not."

She stared back at him without responding.

He smiled. "Contrary to the apparently prevailing wisdom, it is significantly more difficult to carry on a conversation with someone in the throes of maidenly vapors than it is with a woman in full possession of her faculties."

"Witness the poor rakehell," Camellia murmured. "Reduced to mere *conversations* until his forty days are through and he can return to phi-landering."

To her surprise, a touch of pink graced the earl's chiseled cheekbones.

"The wager," he said, his mouth grim. "Of course."

She made no reply. Sharp words would cause a scene neither of them would want.

Fortunately, her sisters' bonnets were bent together in hushed whispers a few feet ahead, and they had not yet noticed the unwanted interloper in their midst.

"Would you believe the wager had slipped my mind entirely?" he asked.

"No," she said flatly as the crowd inched forward.

"Perhaps not *entirely*," Lord Wainwright admitted. "But it hasn't been at the forefront of my thoughts in days."

She arched a skeptical brow. "Then how have you been staying out of scandal columns?"

"By accident, I suppose. A product of having something else on my mind." His gaze softened, focused not on her but some pleasant memory. A happy sigh escaped his lips.

Camellia tilted her head in surprise. His dreamy expression made her believe he was thinking about some*one* rather than some*thing*. And if there was a woman out there who could put a look that smitten on the face of a rakehell that heartless...

She stared at him in wonder. Perhaps people

could change. Perhaps *she* could change. Hope stirred within her. Beautiful, rebellious hope.

Her lips parted. She wanted more from life than to watch from the wainscoting. Perhaps she was now strong enough to tell her unwanted suitor she would not be entering into a betrothal. How could she? Life was too important to spend it with the wrong person.

In fact, when next she saw Lord X, if he teased her again about slipping off into the shadows for a passionate embrace…

This time, she would not tell him no.

CHAPTER 16

*D*espite standing in the center of a wide, vaulted chamber, Boney's battered blue carriage was almost completely obscured by the dense crowd of eager Londoners swarming about the vermilion wheels and painted panels like bees buzzing about a hive.

Michael was not one of them.

He stood in the far corner, near the tall side windows, his focus not on the spectacle before him, but lost deep in thought.

"Lord Wainwright, Lord Wainwright!"

A quartet of giggling, blushing debutantes fluttered their eyes at him over their painted fans as if they were in the ballroom at Almack's rather than crowded walkway between Napoleon's washbasin and bedstead.

"Ladies." Michael gave as elegant a bow as the cramped space permitted. "I trust you are enjoying the exhibition?"

They tittered at each other as if the question

had been the most amusing anecdote ever spoken.

A stern-faced matron strode up behind them and marched the girls a safe distance away before any of the chits could swoon into Boney's toilette box.

Michael didn't mind silly young ladies. He supposed there might have been a time when any gentleman had once been an equally silly young lad.

After his conversation with Miss Grenville, he wasn't entirely certain he had managed to outgrow the phase.

Addressing her had been spontaneous... and, perhaps, ill-advised. But she had been standing not a hand's width in front of him amidst a queue as long as the Serpentine, and he had just thought...

Had he thought? Of course she would be stand-offish. The sum total of their prior interactions had included him calling her sister a termagant, Miss Grenville inventing burn-in-hell Bible verses to shame him, followed by a heated exchange at the circus.

The back of his neck heated. He had never before made such a muck of simple encounters, and he hoped never to repeat the experience. No wonder Miss Grenville believed him incapable of comporting himself properly for forty days.

He had been speaking the truth when he told her he'd forgotten about the wager. Not that he didn't want to win. He *had* to win. 'Twas simply that, since the night he'd met Lady X, she had become all he could think about. He hadn't even danced with another woman since, much less flirted with anyone else.

He acknowledged the irony. He hadn't had to try very hard to stay out of the scandal columns— his obsession with Lady X had achieved that for him.

Although there *had* been a few near misses. Particularly when there was a Grenville about. They had good reason to dislike him. He ran a hand through his hair in dismay.

Until the wager, he hadn't given much thought to how others perceived him. Michael had always done his best to compliment every lady and befriend all the gentlemen simply because he liked *people*, not because he sought any particular reward or notoriety. But things didn't always go as one wished.

"Mmm, if it isn't the earl," cooed a female voice behind his ear. "My favorite flavor."

Bloody hell, not the widow Epworth on one of her relentless prowls. Blast. Michael heroically refrained from fleeing through the closest exit.

"Mrs. Epworth." He kept his tone pleasant but distant. "Are you enjoying Napoleon's carriage?"

She licked her lips. "I would enjoy the view far more if you and I were in the back, taking full advantage of that plush satin squab."

Michael edged slightly to one side. Say what one would about the widow Epworth, she certainly didn't waste time making one guess where her interests lay.

"I am afraid I shall have to decline your generous offer."

"Too public a place? My townhouse is much more private. You should pay me a visit. It's been years since last we… 'talked.'" She gave a suggestive, open-mouthed wink, lest he not have quite followed the subtleties of her innuendo.

He tried to think of a demurral that would neither offend her sensibilities nor intrigue her into trying harder to ensnare him. "I'm afraid I am no longer on the market."

"Pish-posh. A leopard cannot change its spots. Nor would I wish you to." She turned away, only to blow him a kiss over her shoulder. "You know where to find me when you change your mind."

Once, a comment like that would not have bothered him. Indeed, in Michael's younger days, he had gone so far as to cultivate a debonair, rakish demeanor. He hadn't minded at all that his harmless flirtations and pleasurable assignations had garnered him a dashing but scandalous reputation as an accomplished rake.

After all, his actions with respectable young ladies had always been those of a gentleman. And his activities with the demimonde had always been mutually desirable. Women like Mrs. Epworth were already "fallen." Everyone won. He was a bachelor, he was rich, he was titled—gossip was just noise, not something that actually mattered.

Except perhaps it did.

The Grenville sisters had clearly found him lacking. Unlike the rest of the ton, Miss Grenville didn't find the wager a jolly spot of fun at all. She thought him worse than scandalous. She believed him to be heartless. A cad.

He frowned. What would his mystery lady think? It hadn't mattered because outside of the masquerade, they were strangers. But what if he did discover her name, or she his? He had indulged fantasies about seeing her again, of being with each other as their true selves.

But what if his overblown reputation was simply too scandalous for that to be possible? Michael's fingers went cold. What if he told her that she was all he ever thought about... and she didn't believe him?

He ground his teeth in frustration. On the surface, his past history spoke for itself. His affections rarely lasted longer than an evening—because the women who had lain with him had not expected anything more. He, too, was often little more than a fling to boast about.

His jaw set. Regardless of what Miss Grenville and her sisters might believe, he had never seduced an innocent. London contained too many experienced women who knew exactly what they wanted for him to risk getting too close to a marriageable female. With the demimonde, even knowing each other's names was superfluous. Why pretend either party had designs on the future?

Except now he did pretend. He dreamed about sharing many more moments with Lady X, in the bedchamber and out. He wanted to kiss her lips at the bank of her river, just as they'd imagined when he'd held her in his arms on the stone folly beneath the stars.

The fantasy was delightful, but no longer sufficed. They were capable of so much more. If he could only divine her real name…

Would their blossoming romance have a chance outside of the masquerade? Or would it all come crashing down about them?

The damp edge of a wet parasol snagged the tail of his coat.

"Lord Wainwright! I beg your pardon. I was so startled by the stuffed birds on the shelf behind the carriage that I didn't see where I was going." A young lady turned slowly scarlet beneath the brim of her bonnet.

He bowed. "Why, good afternoon Miss Digby. There is nothing at all to forgive. I myself was just wondering what brilliant artist had decided stuffed beasts needed to be displayed in metal cages. One should hope we're in no danger of them coming back to life."

"Never fear," Miss Digby whispered. "I am armed. If they attack, I shall strike them with my wet parasol."

He gave a delicate shudder. "I myself live in fear of the unpredictable nature of your majestic parasol. The stuffed beasts haven't a chance."

She grinned and tucked the instrument safely

out of harm's way. "Thank you for being so kind. I trust I have left no lasting damage?"

"Only to my pride," he assured her. "Enjoy the exhibition, Miss Digby."

"You as well, Lord Wainwright." She bobbed a curtsy before disappearing into the crowd.

Michael tried to return his attention to Boney's carriage. For as long as he'd stood in the exhibition hall, he had yet to examine the luxurious spoils of war.

Yet his gaze went not to the Imperial arms and gold candlesticks, but to the eldest Grenville sister. From the corner of his eye, it appeared the trio were making their way toward the exit.

He pushed back his shoulders in determination. He had been out of sorts in more ways than one these past few weeks, and the middle sister had suffered for it. Despite the horrendous day he'd had, despite the inexplicable vehemence she'd displayed to him from out of nowhere, a gentleman should not snap at a lady.

Perhaps this was the perfect moment to apologize for insulting her. Michael straightened his beaver hat and hurried outside, a hopeful smile playing at his lips. They could finally put the awkwardness behind them.

He caught up with the sisters just as they were hailing a hackney. "Ladies, if you could grant a brief moment, I believe I owe one of you an apology."

All three women stared back at him with identical blank expressions, as if he were not an infamous earl but a forgettable servant whose function they could not recall.

See? No rancor this time. He was positively growing on them.

He swept off his hat and faced the middle sister. "I apologize for the thoughtless words before your dinner party. There is no excuse for such rudeness. I should never have called you a termagant."

"Of course there's an excuse," she said with a sigh. "You would never have reacted thus, had I not called you a soulless cretin and implied you couldn't read."

Michael blinked in surprise.

"I provoked you. I meant to." She winced at the memory. "It was not at all well done of me, but I was just so *angry* with you…"

"Angry with me?" He tried to think. "For requesting you refrain from whinnying at my soirée?"

"Not the whinnying." She waved an impatient hand. "I can whinny anytime I wish. What I cannot do every time I wish is raise funds to cover the operating costs of my school for wayward girls. Without sufficient donations, dozens of young ladies will find themselves back on the streets, back in the nightmarish environments they've only just escaped."

He frowned at the sudden shift in topic. "It sounds like a worthy cause."

"It is. That's why I was furious with you for ruining it."

He stepped backward in surprise. "*I* ruined it? This is the first I've heard of it."

"That is the point." Her smile was brittle. "One month ago, I presented the charity opportunity to an interested group of socially conscious society ladies at the Blaylock soirée. All had previously expressed their intent to donate funds once they learned more about the project."

"That sounds wonderful," he said hesitantly. "I don't see how I—"

"You interrupted our gathering, complimented the ladies on their beauty and accomplishments, and cautioned them to beware creating more competition." She pulled a face. "I presumed you were jesting. The others did not. Every single promised donation was rescinded the moment you left."

His stomach sank in horror. He didn't recall the conversation in question. He wasn't even certain what night it might have been.

But, to his chagrin, he could not claim to be surprised. He attended so many events, greeted countless people. The words were automatic.

Michael had always believed the only sane way of managing innumerable social interactions was to be kind to all guests and keep the conversation superficial. Admire a gentleman's new hunting box, compliment the embroidery on a lady's reticule. He had been trying to avoid problems, not to create one for someone else.

"I didn't mean…" he began.

She lifted a shoulder. "I know. My sister

186

pointed out that was likely the case. Yet the consequences remain the same."

He swung his gaze to the eldest Grenville. The one who had quoted false testament at him in Hyde Park and later expelled him from her house and onto his ear after overhearing his remarks to her sister. He could not blame her.

His throat grew thick. She hadn't thrown him out because of his thoughtless comment in the midst of his foul mood. She'd thrown him out because it was one more straw in an endless stream of slights. From him, from the world at large. She'd thrown him out because she *could*. Because their home was the one place she and her sisters had any say at all.

"I apologize," he said again, though words had never once solved anything. He hoped they realized he spoke the truth. "I won't keep you any longer. Enjoy the rest of your day."

The two youngest sisters mounted the step into the hackney and disappeared inside without taking their leave. The elder Miss Grenville gazed at him for a moment longer before doing the same.

He stared back at the blank dusty walls as the door swung closed and the hack rattled away. Miss Grenville's silent gaze had unsettled him for reasons he could not say.

Perhaps because unlike the rest of society, she did not see him as a rake to be reformed or a bachelor to be won. Nor did she see him as the empty-headed Adonis depicted in the caricatures.

ERICA RIDLEY

Miss Grenville didn't give a damn about his title or his money. Her sensible heart didn't flutter at the thought of hearing her name on his lips or having him press a kiss to her gloved hand. She cared about things that mattered. Like sticking up for other people. Like taking care of her family.

He had meant his apology. The Grenville sisters might not trust his sincerity. He would not blame them for skepticism. But he would do everything within his power to ensure he was never so careless with how his words might affect someone else again.

Michael snugged his beaver hat back onto his head and strode to his carriage. As soon as he returned home, he would have his man of business determine which bank held the account for the school, and ensure an anonymous deposit was made forthwith.

If there was one thing that was certain after today, it was that the pleasure-seeker he had once been was not the man he wished to be. Not for the Grenville sisters, not for Lady X, and not for himself. The future had changed course, and he wanted Lady X to be part of it.

He was not merely out to win a wager. He was out to win a countess.

CHAPTER 17

*D*ays later, Michael strode through the flower garden at the rear of his property and wondered how it might fare in the eyes of Lady X.

He had been mooning over her for the better part of a week. It had become such a normal part of his daily routine that could scarcely remember what life had been like before she had overtaken his every waking thought.

Nor did he wish to return to those whirlwind but meaningless days. He wanted more of his nights with Lady X. He wanted her here, at his home. In his arms. At his breakfast table. The hours they spent together at each masquerade were delightful beyond compare, but he wanted... *more*.

He wished he were not strolling through the twisting paths of his garden alone. But what could he do?

The next time he saw Lady X, should he ask

for her name? Or was the wisest path to continue as things were, for as long as she'd let him?

Uncertainty itched beneath his skin. He didn't want to push too hard and send her running. But he also didn't want to wait too long and lose her anyway.

There was no right answer. Only two risky choices with unknowable outcomes.

Frustrated with his mad obsession over a woman whose name he didn't know, he had spent the past several days trying to distract himself from the mystery of Lady X.

Since the last masquerade, Michael had visited Bullock's Museum for the carriage exhibit and Cribb's Parlour in Haymarket the next day for bare-knuckle boxing. Then half a bottle of Blue Ruin at the Daffy Club. After regretting that decision intensely the following morning, he had shoved down the brim of his hat to block the sun from his bloodshot eyes and met a few friends at the Peerless Pool. He took daily walks just like this one hoping to queer his blue devils.

Nothing worked. He was positively smitten. Nothing could quit Lady X from his mind.

Frustrated, he turned away from his garden and headed toward the mews at the rear. His pace increased in determination. Friends would be a good distraction. He summoned his coach and set out for the Cloven Hoof.

As Mayfair slowly disappeared from the carriage's side windows, Michael did his very best not to imagine himself en route to Lady X's

London domicile, wherever it might be, with flowers or imported chocolates in hand. This was not the right time.

Before he did anything rash, he had to win his wager.

The fact that Lady X had let slip that she must take great care to guard her reputation hinted at her social standing… and her priorities. Michael had to win this bet not just to prove himself to his friends, as he'd first intended, but to prove himself to society at large. Especially Lady X.

If he could not manage forty days without scandal, she would never think of him as anything more than a rakehell. A temporary lover with whom a lady might pass a few pleasurable hours before finding a serious gentleman more worthy of her time.

He wanted to be worthy of her time. More than that, he wanted to be worthy of her heart. Or at least to hope for the possibility of winning it. He didn't want to offer her a future filled with caricatures and whispered gossip. He wanted to offer a life she could enjoy. A home she could relax in. A man she could trust.

He wanted her to want him as much as he wanted her.

As soon as the carriage ceased moving, he leapt from the cab to the paved stone below and strode into the dimly lit interior of the Cloven Hoof.

Clumps of men with intense expressions and half full glasses of brandy crowded the gaming tables. The bar was empty save for a serving girl arranging drinks on a tray. Michael glanced up toward the ceiling.

The caricatures those blackguards Gideon and Hawkridge had so helpfully strung up like Christmas decorations rustled in the breeze from the closing door. Although sun and soot now rendered the printed etchings illegible, Michael's friends had likely left them up just to needle him.

It worked, damn them.

He found both scoundrels at a rear table. From their shadowed corner, they had an excellent view of the bar, the gaming tables, and the front door.

By size of their grins, they had both witnessed him glance up at the ceiling the moment he crossed the threshold. He allowed his irritation to show on his face. The rotters were enjoying this wager entirely too much.

He slid into the seat opposite Gideon, viciously pleased the strung etchings had since faded to blurs. He hoped his past soon would, too.

Some of the drawings Michael supposed he had deserved. He was indeed a shameless flirt. He did, in fact, love wine, music, and people of all walks of life. Perhaps he was the "Lord of Pleasure."

But the other caricatures, the truly hurtful ones, had not been earned. He had never cuckolded a friend—or anyone at all. There was no secret chamber of debauchery hidden within his house. His thoughts while in the House of Lords were not on women, as the artists depicted, but rather the very real problems of the day.

There was a time and a place for being derelict. Parliament was not that place. Michael's vote carried the same weight as any other, and he did his best to ensure he used it wisely.

Perhaps now that his name wasn't splashed across every scandal column in England, he might finally develop a reputation he could be proud of.

"Wainwright." Gideon motioned for one of the serving girls to bring an extra glass. "Haven't seen you in over three weeks. How is the wager coming?"

"The fact that you have to ask means you know I'm winning," Michael said as he accepted a glass of brandy.

Gideon laughed. "You're not *winning*. You're twenty-five days into a forty-day wager."

"Twenty-four days longer than I had him pegged for." Lord Hawkridge lifted his glass. "A toast to you, Wainwright. Whether you make it to day forty or not."

Michael tried not to let his irritation show. "I'll make it far past day forty. I don't intend for my name to return to the scandal columns at all."

Gideon arched a dark brow. "Shall I fetch the betting book?"

"Amusing," Michael said through clenched teeth. "I'm in earnest."

"I'm in dire straits," Lord Hawkridge put in. "That's a wager I would take."

Michael set down his glass. He loved his friends, but the jests at his expense had lost their humor. He shoved a hand through his hair in frustration.

If he ever had been the dashing but frivolous rake depicted in the caricatures, he was not the same man now. Thanks to the Grenville sisters, he had a new respect for the impact "meaning-less" words could have on others.

Thanks to Lady X, words held more than mere meaning. Their long, candid conversations on everything from family to society expectations to dreams of the future connected them on a level he hadn't realized possible. The best nights of his life had not been hunting conquests on a dance floor, but strolling beneath the stars with Lady X.

"Take your wagers," he enunciated, "and shove them up your—"

"Ah." Gideon's smile was wide. "There's a woman."

Michael started in surprise. "How do you know?"

Gideon lifted a shoulder with a knowing ex-pression in his eyes. "What else could make a rakehell wish to be a better man?"

"Fair enough." Michael didn't bother trying to deny it. With any luck, his connection with Lady X would not have to remain secret for long. He swirled the brandy in his glass, then looked up at his friends. "Have you ever been in love?"

"Don't believe in love," Gideon answered without hesitation. He used his glass to gesture at the gaming tables behind him. "I don't believe in anything but money."

"I'm not sure I believe in money," Lord Hawkridge said drily. "It's been so long since I saw any. As much as I do believe in love, I cannot afford it. My best hope is an heiress who can stand my company long enough to beget an heir."

"And a spare," Gideon reminded him. "It would be dreadful not to have multiple hungry mouths to bequeath your destitute marquessate to."

Lord Hawkridge cut him a flat look. "*Heiress*, I said. They tend to come with dowries. Veritable pots of precious gold."

"If you find one. You *say* you'll wed for money," Gideon granted, "but anyone who believes in something as ephemeral as love cannot be trusted with matters of the heart."

Hawkridge ignored him and turned his pointed gaze back to Michael. "What about you, Wainwright? Will you wed for love or for the earldom?"

Michael stared back at him wordlessly. Although he had no lack of finances, Michael had always supposed he'd marry for the earldom, not for love.

Not just anyone could be a countess. The position required the right woman. A virginal paragon of excellent breeding, impeccable manners, the right connections. It was an earl's duty. Michael had always known the title came before personal considerations.

For the first time he wondered not whether Lady X would accept him—but whether he would be able to accept her. What if she were a dressmaker? A courtesan? A performer at the theater? It hadn't occurred to him to worry about her pedigree. But what type of women attended Lambley's masquerades? He doubted it was the sort that later went on to become countesses. Upper class women would not risk their future for a masked gala.

Michael rubbed his face. He had let himself obsess for nothing. She was a mystery, and would have to remain one. Lord help him, he could not afford to fall in love with someone he couldn't wed. It was better to never know her name at all. He would spend as much time with her as the Fates allowed, but he would not push for anything more than the masquerades offered.

Probably.

His fingers clenched inside his pockets. He was already half in love, damn his foolish hide. But it didn't signify. His obsession with Lady X would stay in the shadows where it belonged.

After the Season was over and the masquerades ceased, they were unlikely to see each other again. A dull disappointment spread through his limbs at the realization. The loss of her company would be a severe blow. He would remember their shared nights for the rest of his life.

But for the rest of his days, he would do well to recall that he was not Lord X, but Lord Wainwright. Guardian of an earldom. Representative in the House of Lords.

He should focus not on fantasies, but on his responsibilities. When the Season ended, it would indeed be time to find a countess worthy of the title.

Lady X would simply have to remain his favorite memory.

CHAPTER 18

*C*amellia did not hurry from the hired hack toward Lambley's ducal residence, but rather took each slow, measured step with a renewed sense of awareness and freedom.

Before, she had slipped away with Lord X for stolen moments, knowing full well she could let things progress no further than heated kisses, because she would soon be betrothed to another man.

Tonight was different. *She* was different. When Mr. Bost returned to finalize his paperwork with her father, Camellia would force both men to understand that future was not a path she would be pursuing.

If it meant remaining a spinster for the rest of her days, so be it. At least she would be free. Free of expectations, free of guilt. Free to explore her relationship with Lord X wherever it might lead. Free to fall in love. Free to walk away.

It wasn't until she stepped inside the duke's

antechamber and removed her emerald feather mask that she realized she'd forgotten to acquire a new codeword to use in lieu of a proper invitation. Nor could she use Lord X as a reference, because she didn't even know his name. Her cheeks flamed.

She stuttered in embarrassment. "I'm afraid I haven't a proper invitation, but I'm... friends with..."

"Everyone, of course." The doorkeeper's smile was genuine as he motioned for her to retie her mask. "The duke has a permanent place for you on his list of regular attendees. You're welcome here anytime."

Wonder filled her. A permanent place on the list of regulars! A grin curved her lips as she straightened her shoulders.

For the first time, she felt like the night truly did belong to her.

The doorkeeper swept open the door from the vestibule to the hall of merrymakers. "Lady X, my friends!"

"Lady X!" the crowd shouted back in delight.

Before she could take so much as a step, strong hands swung her into a familiar embrace.

"I have been standing by this doorway since a quarter till ten," Lord X scolded in his warm, husky voice.

She arched a brow. "The doors don't even open until ten."

"I was first." He stole a quick kiss before letting her out of his embrace.

She missed his warmth immediately and looped her arm through his. "First? Just you alone in an empty ballroom?"

"I would have arrived straight after breakfast, had Lambley not instructed his man not to let me in until a reasonable approximation of the proper hour." Lord X's tone was teasing, but his expression was hidden behind the inky feathers of his ebony mask.

"Why so early?" she asked. "You had to know no one else would be here yet."

"I don't care about anyone else. I care about you." He leaned close. "I missed you terribly, no matter how hard I tried not to. It was horrid. Quite shameful of you to tie up a man's heartstrings so callously."

Pleasure filled her rather than remorse. "I didn't do it on purpose, you know."

"I do know. That's why it worked. If you had *meant* to ensnare me, I would have slipped the noose. As it stands, I didn't even notice the gradual loss of air until you had stolen the breath from my lungs completely."

"What a dreadful analogy," she laughed as she playfully straightened his cravat. "I should hope our interactions are nothing like a trip to the gallows."

"Only in the sense that I'm falling," he replied, his tone cryptic. "Where are we off to tonight? The promenade? The garden?"

"Tonight, I wish to dance." She wished to do everything she'd been too frightened to try before. She wanted to be free.

He glanced upstairs. "To the roof?"

She shook her head. Last time, she had barely been brave enough to dance in private. This time, she was bold enough to let the entire world see. She wasn't a wallflower anymore, or any other limiting label.

"Right here." She was Lady X. And she wanted to dance.

Perhaps she'd even steal a kiss in the middle of the ballroom.

He led her into the chamber with the orchestra and onto the parquet floor. "May I have this waltz, Lady X?"

"I'm yours for the rest of the night." She smiled up at him. Hadn't stopped smiling, in fact, since the moment the doorkeeper welcomed her to the masquerade. She was utterly, deliriously happy. Tonight was going to be perfect.

Lord X lifted her right hand in his and curved his other arm about her waist as he expertly led her about the dance floor in time to the music.

Her pulse raced with every dip and twirl as she swirled through the crowd of masked revelers in the safety and excitement of his arms.

"You look ravishing tonight," he murmured into her ear. "Every time I see you, you're even more beautiful than the last, but in that emerald gown... Every woman here tonight wishes she were you, and every gentleman wishes he were me. I might be the most fortunate man alive."

Her cheeks heated behind her feather mask.

Had anyone ever envied her before? Tonight, they should. She had Lord X and she had no intention of letting him go.

"Thank you," she said softly over the thumping of her heart.

She *felt* beautiful tonight. The shimmering emerald silk of her dress, the sparkling teardrops of her earrings, the faux diamonds adorning the cat-eye cutouts of her scarlet-plumed mask. Even her satin slippers were new, cradling her feet in luxurious softness.

In Lord X's arms, she soared and dipped in tandem with the music of the orchestra, as if the flutes and violins played not for the masquerade but solely for the two of them.

Though his expression was hidden behind the black feathers of his mask, the focus and intensity of Lord X's gaze had never once wavered from Camellia. It was as if, as it was for her, everyone else had ceased to exist.

The champagne-drunk merrymakers, the thousands of shimmering candles in the chandeliers overhead, the night itself was naught but a buoyant blur, serving only as an excuse to remain locked in each other's arms.

Not that any excuse was required. The opposite! She could not imagine willfully leaving his embrace. Every moment in his arms only made her long for another, and another. A waltz was merely a prelude to a kiss, each kiss merely a promise of something more.

And, oh, did she want more. She yearned to

feel the warmth of his hands not only on the curve of her spine but on *all* of her curves. Every inch of her trembled with wanting to feel his touch, his tongue, his kiss.

When he pulled her close to brush his lips against the lobe of her ear, the base of her neck, 'twas all she could do not to melt into his arms and beg him to steal her away to a private nook. Somewhere their tantalizing kisses need not be teasing hints of forbidden pleasure but rather only the beginning of a passion too incendiary to deny.

When at last the waltz ended, the orchestra set aside their instruments for a brief intermission. The other merrymakers deserted the now silent ballroom.

Lord X stole a long slow kiss, then tucked her hand against his arm. "Shall we watch the stars from the roof? Escape to the garden to walk amongst the flowers? Or should we find our magic elsewhere?"

"Elsewhere," she said without hesitation. Before she could change her mind, she twined her arms about his neck and pressed her body to his with a kiss so passionate it threatened to consume her entire soul. For this one perfect night, she would be his. "Let's make our own magic."

CHAPTER 19

*C*amellia kept her arms wrapped tight about Lord X's neck as he carried her into a darkened chamber. The embers of a faint fire cast a small section of the interior in a soft glow.

He kicked the door shut behind them and laid her in the center of a large, soft bed before dashing back to the door to ensure the lock was engaged.

The wide, arched bedchamber was bathed in too much shadow to discern anything but the smudge of orange within the fireplace. Even colors had disappeared, making her deep emerald gown almost as charcoal black as Lord X's tail-coat and breeches.

Voluptuous darkness bathed them in even richer anonymity than mere masks could provide, yet simultaneously grounded her more fully in the moment. Being unable to see only heightened her other senses. The luxurious softness of the bed, the heady sandalwood scent of his cologne, the firmness of his warm lips as they sought hers.

She required no coaxing to respond in kind. Every part of her reached for him, drawing him closer with her arms, drinking him in with her mouth, with her every breath. She thrilled at the weight of his tall, lithe body pressed into hers atop the feather mattress.

He was so solid, so warm, so big. Everything about him was larger than life. Harder, hotter, *better* than she had even dreamed. She never wanted the evening to end. He drew his kisses ever lower, from her mouth to the sensitive area just below the lobe of her ear, from the pulse point at the base of her neck to the curves of her breasts just above the scandalous dip of her bodice.

Heart thumping, she arched into his touch, pressing her bare flesh toward the tantalizing heat of his mouth in sensual abandon. It was as if the past four weeks of soul-baring conversation and whirlwind romance had led them to this place, this moment. For this one perfect night, she would be his and he would be hers.

She longed to sink her fingers into his hair, but did not want to risk dislodging his mask. Tonight was not about who they were to the world, but rather who they were to each other. They could no more stop this moment than they could stop the sun from rising.

An incredible sense of happiness, of peace, of

ERICA RIDLEY

life finally being utterly and completely *right* flooded her with joy and confidence. This was who she was meant to be. Who she was meant to be with.

Her eyelids fluttered in mindless pleasure as he closed his mouth over her breast and teased the straining nipple with his expert tongue. She wanted more. The thin silk of her gown was too great an impediment, the many layers of his tailcoat and waistcoat and undershirt unnecessary barriers between them.

She tugged loose his cravat from his neck, fumbled at the buttons hiding him from her touch. As if reading her thoughts, he lifted his mouth from her trembling body only long enough to shuck his tailcoat to the floor, his waistcoat, his billowing linen undershirt.

His bare flesh was hot to the touch, thrilling and forbidden. She ran her hands over the hard planes of his stomach, the rippling muscle of his strong arms, his wide shoulders, his back. The encompassing darkness around them made her feel all the more present, his body and his kisses all the more real.

She twisted in his embrace, exposing the silk-covered buttons along her spine.

Rather than make quick work of the short row of buttons, he deliberately took his time, loosening each small button with aching tenderness. He pressed a reverent kiss to each new inch of flesh he uncovered, as if he was unwrapping the most precious package he'd ever been given.

She shivered in pleasure at each touch. He did not make her feel merely desired, but beloved. As if he had been waiting for her his entire life.

When at last the final button slipped free, her silk gown fluttered to her hips. Rather than immediately retake her reclining position against the pillows, she slid from the bed to kneel at Lord X's feet. With him, she did not feel naked, but alive. She wanted him to feel the same.

With the same care he had shown her emerald gown, she unlaced his boots and tugged them free. She set them aside, set her slippers aside, let her gown flutter to her feet.

Only her shift remained, its ivory linen so thin it would be nearly transparent if it were visible in the darkness. Instead of using their eyes, they discovered each other's bodies with their hands, explored with their mouths, tasted with their tongues.

He lowered her shift over her shoulders and hips and laid her back against the soft pillows.

Now she wore nothing but her feather mask and a pair of thigh-high silk stockings that somehow felt even more decadent against the heat of his flesh than bare skin would have done.

Pulse racing, she reached up for the buttons at the fall of his breeches. Before her fingers could do more than graze the hard muscle of his abdomen, he knelt between her silk stockings and lowered his mouth to her core.

A stuttering gasp escaped her lips at the unexpected, overwhelming pleasure building deep inside her with every intoxicating lick of his tongue. It was impossible, wonderful, all-encompassing.

His fingers joined his tongue, driving inexorably within her as his mouth stoked her fire higher and higher. She abandoned herself wholly to sensation as wave after wave of dizzying pleasure rocked through her.

Only when her legs ceased their trembling did he lift his mouth from between her legs.

Drunk with desire, she reached for him. He returned his open-mouthed kisses to her breasts, her sensitive nipples, and settled himself between her thighs.

Within seconds, the delicious invasion of his thick member pressing into her went from pleasure to pain and she cried out in shock.

He froze at the sound, his body so perfectly still it was as if time itself ceased to flow around them.

"You're…" he managed weakly, the rest of the sentence lost amongst the strangled syllables in his throat.

A virgin. Yes. She had been, anyway. Was glad not to be anymore. Was thrilled it was here, with him. She wrapped her legs about his hips, coaxing him in further.

"Do it," she whispered into his neck. "I want you to."

"I think I already did." He remained motionless, as if afraid any additional movement might break her. "I didn't know you hadn't…"

"Now I have." She tilted her hips toward his, forcing him to slide deeper within her. A sense of feminine power flooded her as a guttural moan of pleasure escaped his lips. "Please don't stop. I want you. I want *this*."

"Then this isn't over," he said as he sank himself fully within her. "Not tonight. Not ever." His muscles flexed with every thrust inside her. "From this moment on, you are mine."

Her body contracted about him as he staked his claim over and over with each long, demanding stroke of his hot, hard member. He locked his fingers with hers, pinning her hands to either side of her head.

"Mine," he repeated as his hips bucked faster, rocking into her again and again. "Say it."

"Yours," she gasped against his shoulder as a second wave of ecstasy took her. Her hips rose to meet him even as her legs trembled helplessly in shocks of pleasure.

"*Forever.*" He gave a last, shuddering thrust and collapsed half on top of her, spent.

Her pulse pounded in time with his, the fingers of their hands still twined together as they gasped for breath.

He pressed his lips to her temple in a sweet, exhausted kiss.

Somewhere on the opposite side of the chamber from the main corridor, a door swung open. Camellia's heart stopped at the unexpected sound. God save her. This bedchamber had *servant access*. Mortification swallowed her whole.

Of course there was servant access. This was a ducal residence, after all.

Voices and candlelight spilled into the room as whoever had been in the adjoining room crossed the threshold into theirs.

Camellia froze with her bare legs locked about Lord X's equally bare hips. Terror rushed through her as merrymakers swept in like a tidal wave.

"Knock me over with a feather," came a shrill, laughing voice. "I'd recognize those handsome buttocks anywhere. One never forgets the strawberry-shaped birthmark of the Lord of Pleasure. Though I can't say I recognize the shapely lady beneath you."

Terror stole the air from Camellia's lungs.

"Bloody hell." He lowered his head as if to hide his masked face in her hair. "Please don't let that be Mrs. Epworth."

Camellia froze as reality cut through the fog of their lovemaking. The notoriously promiscuous Mrs. Epworth had recognized Lord X from a birthmark on his buttocks? Her entire body shook with fear and confusion. Humiliation engulfed her.

"What's that?" the widow cooed loudly in reply. "Are we interrupting your pleasure? Pay no attention to us, Wainwright. We'll let ourselves back out the way we came in—and we'll lock the door behind us."

Wainwright? Camellia shoved him off her in a flood of panic, her heart fluttering in horror. Heaven help her. She'd given her maidenhead to

Lord Wainwright? Her throat gagged at the abhorrent thought.

The connecting door snicked shut, taking the observers—and the source of light—with them. Her body sprang to life.

Pulse racing in fear and panic, she threw herself blindly from the bed in search of her shift. It had to be here. Somewhere. She had to get away. Right *now*. Had to get out of this masquerade, out of this building, out of this costume and into a piping hot bath from which she might never leave.

"Lady X?" A hesitant stammer marred the familiar husky voice.

She yanked her gown over her head, shoved her arms through the sleeves. Lord Wainwright might think himself just as discomfited by the unexpected interruption as she was, but the devil knew he couldn't even come close.

He cleared his throat from the other side of the bed. "Lady X, I'm…"

"Lord Wainwright," she interrupted harshly, still unable to believe the depths of her folly. "I heard."

"Yes, well… guilty on that count, I'm afraid. But it changes nothing. I swear it."

He was wrong. It changed everything.

She grappled for her satin slippers and tugged them onto her feet as quickly as possible.

"At least tell me your name," he said, his tone desperate. "I meant everything I said, everything I did. I want you to be mine inside these walls and out. You mean… *everything.*"

Camellia had meant it all, too. At the time. But now she knew better.

She had been a fool.

Heat stung her throat. She did not trust herself to open her mouth. Didn't know what she might say if she dared to speak. She hurried to the door while her shaking legs still obeyed her commands. Somehow, her fingers managed to release the lock.

"Please," he begged. "Just your name. You are…?"

"Gone," she answered softly.

Camellia raced from the room, the back of her gaping gown flapping against her bare shoulders, exposing her for the fool she was. Her gaze blurred as she stumbled through the crowd as quickly as she could.

She needed a hack. She needed to get home. She needed to die from humiliation and self-loathing.

Perhaps sensing her desperation, the crowd parted to let her through. Who cared if they noticed the telltale wrinkles in her gown and bed-mussed hair? She wouldn't be back. Ever. She was no longer Lady X.

Now, she was simply ruined.

CHAPTER 20

*M*ichael dashed from the empty bedchamber into the crowded corridor wearing only one of his infernal Hessians, but it was already too late. Lady X was nowhere to be seen. He slammed his fist against the doorjamb in frustration. Damn his unforgivable arrogance.

He'd taken her virginity… and she hadn't even given him her name.

"Looking for someone?" came a coy, laughing voice. The blasted Mrs. Epworth.

Naturally.

He ducked back into the bedchamber and threw himself onto the edge of a chaise longue to yank on his other boot.

The widow followed him inside. "Lose your paramour, darling? I'd be happy to take her place. As I mentioned at the museum, it's been years since we—"

"No," he said curtly as he shoved his arms into his tailcoat.

Either Mrs. Epworth could not discern the vehemence of his glare from behind his feather mask, or she simply did not care.

She dragged the tips of her fingernails along the bed. "Who was that divine creature, darling?"

"Lady X."

He had to find her. Desperation trembled his fingers as he buttoned his waistcoat. He snatched his cravat up from the floor and turned back toward the door.

"Don't be that way," Mrs. Epworth pouted. "You can tell *me* your ladybird's name. I won't breathe a single word."

Michael glared at the unrepentant widow, as irritated with himself as he was with her. How could he divulge Lady X's name to someone else when he hadn't the foggiest notion what it might be?

"Why, look at this exquisite piece of craftsmanship." Mrs. Epworth lifted something from between the pillows. "Never say Lady X lost a glass earring in her flight from your arms?"

He leapt toward the bed and plucked the sparkling jewels from her gloved palm. It was indeed one of the green-and-crystal teardrop earrings Lady X had been wearing. His pulse jumped. He closed his fingers about it for safekeeping and strode toward the door.

"Wait," Mrs. Epworth called from her position

of repose upon the bed. "May I not tempt you into staying? Just once, for old time's sake?"

He paused at the threshold only long enough to glance over his shoulder. "I thank you for promising not to breathe a word of this to anyone."

Whether her offer of silence would last beyond the current hour, however, was anyone's guess.

Although she would be banned from all future masquerades for her loose tongue, the widow might consider it a fair trade. The fame of imparting such delicious gossip would garner her the attention she craved. Invitations to parties where one wasn't required to wear a mask.

Michael ground his teeth. He couldn't worry about that. Not right now. The only thing he cared about was finding Lady X.

With a scowl, he stalked through the lavish corridors full of elegant merrymakers. Some of the masked ladies tipped their champagne glasses as he passed. He barely noticed. Didn't care.

He hadn't been interested in any other women since the day he met Lady X... whose true name he didn't even know, and whose maidenly innocence he'd just taken extreme liberties with.

Damn it. Michael clenched his jaw in frustration.

He had never been with a virgin before. Hadn't realized any such creatures had ever attended the duke's licentious masquerades. The idea boggled.

But he'd meant what he'd told her. What he'd felt at the time, and still felt now. His fingers jerked as he raked them through his hair. After an interruption like that, however, he wasn't certain Lady X would believe him. She might prefer to remain masked from him forever.

He burst out a side door of the ducal residence and ran toward the queue of empty carriages lining the street. One by one, he quizzed each driver to see if anyone had glimpsed a masked beauty in emerald silk dash from the exit.

Three of the drivers told him the same thing: She had climbed inside the first available hack and tore off like the hounds of hell were on her tail. She was long gone.

Michael was too late.

CHAPTER 21

*H*eart pounding, Camellia shivered in the back seat of a hackney cab. Bloody, bloody, bloody misfortune. What was worse—that she had been in bed with the devil, or that he still held her heart?

Her feather mask fell onto her wrinkled lap. She touched her bare cheeks in nameless horror. How long had the ties been loose? Had the mask been sliding down her face as she fled through the crowd of merrymakers? Did any of the revelers recognize her as she ran past them with her gown undone?

Good grief, had *Wainwright* recognized her? What was she supposed to do now?

She twisted in her seat, grappling for purchase on the silk-covered buttons lining the back of her bodice. It was impossible. Her gown simply could not be fastened without the aid of a lady's maid...

Or of the gentleman who had unbuttoned it to begin with.

She slumped against the side of the carriage and covered her face with her hands. Of all the people to fall so recklessly for, why did it have to be Lord Wainwright? Why couldn't it have been... a cobbler, a chimney sweep, anyone else in all of London but the one man she could not abide?

She halted the hack a full block from her home so that her neighbors would not see her race up her front steps with her spine bared to the moonlight. Instead, she hurried through the hedgerows and the shadows and slipped through a servants' entrance at the rear.

Careful not to disturb the sleeping hall boy, she managed to sneak up the stairs and into her private bedchamber without awakening anyone in the household.

But her troubles were far from over. They were just beginning.

She sank onto the padded stool before her vanity table and reached up to remove her teardrop earrings.

One. She only had one. A gasp of panic tangled in her throat.

Then she realized an earring was the least of what she'd lost.

With shaking hands, she tossed her mask and the sole remaining earring onto the vanity and bent her forehead to its otherwise neat surface.

Nothing else in her life was neat or tidy. This was more than a mere pickle. Now she not only had to turn down Mr. Bost's proposal... she couldn't marry anyone, ever. She was *ruined*.

And the one man who should be obligated to take her was the one man she could never accept.

Even if she forgave him for his remarks to her sister, Lord Wainwright would still be the most celebrated and infamous rakehell in all of England. His deeds were as thoughtless as his words.

Camellia's limbs shook. She would rather be a ruined spinster living with her parents into infinity than lie alone inside a sumptuous earldom while her promiscuous husband warmed someone else's bed.

What on earth had she been thinking? Lord Wainwright, of all sinful creatures. The man was such an unrepentant libertine, his naked rear was recognizable by a birthmark she hadn't even spent enough time with him to *see*!

Distraught, Camellia pushed away from her vanity table and threw herself face up onto her bed. She rubbed her face with her hands and wished more than anything that they had never been discovered.

An hour ago, she had believed Lord X to be the most exemplary gentleman in all of London.

An hour ago, baring her soul and her self to him had seemed the most perfectly natural thing she could do.

An hour ago, she had been utterly, recklessly, hopelessly in love.

She rolled over to bury her face in her pillow.

Who was she fooling? She was *still* tied up in knots, blast the wretched man.

The nights they had shared. The bonds they had made. Physical, emotional. The closeness she had felt before she'd known who he was.

Before she'd realized it was all part of a well-practiced game.

Her throat stung. Blast it all, *no*. She would not cry over him. He did not deserve it.

She pushed herself up into a seated position to pluck the pins from her hair, mussed from Wainwright's strong hands as they made love.

Camellia swallowed. Best not think of him, if she could help it. She would concentrate on one moment at a time. Brushing her hair. Readying herself for bed. Facing her looking-glass in the morning. Hoping she had not been recognized in her half-dressed flight from the masquerade.

Her chest tightened until she could barely breathe.

The best she could hope for was not to end up a caricature in the scandal columns and have her one moment of mad passion ruin the lives of the rest of her family.

What had she done?

Panic flooded her anew. She desperately wished she could escape to her river rock. The one tranquil place where she could still find peace and serenity. Forget she'd bedded the Lord of Pleasure. That her mask had fallen even as she fled from her mistake.

But of course she could not. If she had been spotted, if her name was now on everyone's tongues...

Camellia could never leave her house again.

CHAPTER 22

*M*ichael was still awake when dawn snaked between the curtains of his bedchamber. He hadn't been able to sleep. Hadn't been able to turn off his churning mind for even a moment.

All he could think about was how perfect things had been with Lady X... until he'd ruined it. Not by something he had done, but by someone he had been. Long before he'd ever met her.

He groaned and covered his face with his hands. Had he feared his scandalous reputation might frighten Lady X away? Try having a past lover recognize him while *in flagrante delicto*. Because of a strawberry-shaped birthmark on his arse.

His spine curved in guilt and chagrin. He was no longer the careless rake he once was. He didn't want meaningless encounters with temporary lovers. He wanted to make a lifelong commitment. His chest grew tight. If Lady X would still have him.

She must have been as embarrassed as he was by the unexpected turn of events. More so. He rubbed the back of his neck in desperation. She'd made the monumental decision to gift him her virginity, and then all of a sudden—

His stomach soured. Their perfect moment could not possibly have gone worse.

Now that he realized the magnitude of her decision to make love to him, he could not imagine how embarrassed, confused, and furious she must be. He would not be surprised if Lady X believed he considered her nothing more than just another conquest.

She could not be more wrong.

Lady X wasn't the conquest. *He* was. She held his heart in her hands. Nothing would give him more pleasure than being able to court her openly, in the manner in which she deserved. He longed to make their connection a true courtship.

If only he knew who she was. The *real* her.

He wanted more than her name. He wanted her to look into his eyes and see the truth shining back when he told her he loved her. That whoever she was, whatever her background, there could be no more perfect countess than having her share his life.

But how? He had already asked Lambley her identity. The duke either did not know, or refused to say. Which left what?

Fairfax.

Hope expanded Michael's chest. Anthony Fairfax was the doorkeeper at the Duke of Lambley's masquerade balls. He would have to know the identity of Lady X!

Michael leapt from his bed and rang for a bath. The last thing he wished to do was postpone his chat with the doorkeeper, but if there was any chance of meeting Lady X face-to-face this very day, he would need to be presentable. More than presentable—*marriageable*.

He hid his impatience as much as possible as he suffered through an abbreviated version of his valet's primping, then had his driver take him straight to Fairfax's residence.

The doorkeeper was not at home. He and his new wife were promenading in Hyde Park.

Blast.

Michael would never be able to find them whilst ambling slowly along in his stately coach, so he requested his driver take him to the mews instead, where Michael forwent the ponderous carriage in favor of his fastest black steed.

As soon as he had mounted, he raced the stallion through the streets of Mayfair and into the cavalcade of Hyde Park. In haste, he nudged his horse between this landau and that curricle until at last he spied a shiny black barouche with Fairfax and his wife at the reins.

Michael dashed forward on his stallion. "Fairfax!"

"Wainwright." The doorkeeper's hallmark

smile was even brighter with his wife at his side. "Heading to a ride on Rotten Row?"

"I no longer care about such distractions." Michael waved away the idea. He didn't have time for such nonsense. All he cared about was finding Lady X. "You must tell me who the divine creature was in the emerald dress. The one in the scarlet-plumed mask with the diamond eyeholes. I am desperate."

Immediate recognition flashed in Fairfax's eyes, but he shook his head firmly. "I am afraid I cannot help. Privacy is paramount." He hesitated, as if sensing Michael's pain. "If you need to contact a partygoer, you could consider speaking to the party's host."

Michael rubbed the back of his neck and sighed. "He won't tell me. He said you wouldn't either, but I had to try."

Fairfax's gaze was sympathetic, but his stance did not change.

Michael steered his black steed toward the park exit and rode hell for leather toward the Cloven Hoof.

Not because he thought anyone inside would know Lady X's identity. But because he didn't have anywhere else left to go.

He tied his stallion at one of the metal horse posts lining the cobbled street and stalked into the gaming den. This time, Lord Hawkridge did not appear to be present.

Good. Michael could only imagine what the morning caricatures looked like after last's night debacle. Losing the wager, however, paled against losing Lady X. Now he had nothing.

Nothing but one more sordid scandal for the papers.

Michael propped his elbows against the bar and glared at the festive rows of sun-faded caricatures overhead.

Gideon selected a bottle of brandy. "Interesting night?"

"You heard." Michael turned toward the counter with a grimace. "How bad are the scandal columns?"

"Devoid of your name. For now." Gideon pushed a glass of brandy across the bar. "But I run a vice parlor. People have been known to talk."

Michael was less surprised that the owner of a gaming hell had overheard whispers about the events of the masquerade, and more shocked that it wasn't already common knowledge amongst the ton.

Mrs. Epworth must have kept her promise not to breathe a word about the incident. The widow possibly presumed that by having ruined Michael's chances with Lady X—yet taking care not to ruin his chances of winning his wager— Michael might agree to sample more of her charms. He would have to disabuse her of that notion.

In fact… perhaps it was past time to dispel several pernicious rumors at once. He drained the rest of his brandy. This plan would require courage. Or at least the brandy-laced equivalent.

He furrowed his brow. "You say my name wasn't in the papers?"

"Not this morning." Gideon arched a dark brow in question.

Michael sighed. "It will be."

He donned his beaver hat and turned toward the door, head held high with determination. He might be on a fool's mission, but there was nothing left to try. He was a man in love. Lady X ought to know.

She was about to find out.

CHAPTER 23

*C*amellia was apprehensive of joining her sisters for supper. She had spent the entire morning cooped up in her bedchamber with the curtains drawn closed, fearful of what fate the morning's scandal columns would bring. Her heart pounded with nerves as she presented herself in their private parlor.

Nothing. Not a peep. For the moment, her double identity seemed to remain a secret.

"How is your school?" she asked her sister before the subject could turn to the masquerade.

Dahlia's face brightened. "Afloat, I'm happy to report. We received an anonymous donation nearly equal to the one that was lost when Lord Wainwright interrupted the charity meeting."

Camellia's answering smile was brittle. She was thrilled that the school for wayward girls was solvent for the moment. Less thrilled that Lord Wainwright's unintentional gaffe still entered the conversation. The grudge-keeping was wearing thin.

Shock froze her teacup halfway to her lips. Dear heavens, had she just sided with Lord Wainwright instead of her own sister? A horrified gasp escaped her throat.

When had she undergone such a radical change of heart? It certainly hadn't been last night, when his buttocks turned out to be as infamous as the rest of him. She had felt more inclined to a truly biblical smiting than to turning the other cheek.

It must have happened much earlier. Far before she'd discovered Wainwright was Lord X. Camellia returned her teacup to its saucer without taking a sip. Seen with objective eyes, rather than protective sister eyes, were his crimes against her family so grave?

He had apologized to Dahlia wholly on his own, and had seemed truly dismayed he had caused such harm with a careless word. The sole occasion in which he had purposefully spoken ill of her sister, Dahlia had provoked his remark by insulting him far more rudely than any person could be expected to bear in silence.

Not that Dahlia would see things that way. She had always viewed the world as black and white. Her strong constitution allowed her to cleave to a moral compass that perhaps wasn't completely aligned with that of society, but always had the greatest amount of good at heart.

No matter his motives or lack thereof, Dahlia

was unlikely to forgive the earl for jeopardizing the futures of two dozen indigent girls.

Just like she would never forgive her sister if she ever found out Camellia had compounded the earl's villainy by sharing a bed with him.

"How was the masquerade?" Bryony asked, eyes sparkling with interest.

"Fine." Camellia's voice cracked weakly on the lie. She shoved a lemon cake into her mouth to prevent any unanswerable questions.

After all, what could she say? She now lived in a glass house. There was no honor in criticizing the earl's nocturnal proclivities when she herself was no better. Camellia's chin lowered. She'd engaged in the most salacious activities *with* him.

They were exactly the same.

A footman swept into the parlor bearing the afternoon paper on a silver tray.

"Thank you, John." Bryony accepted the offering and shook out the paper.

Camellia tried not to sink through her cushioned stool.

"Well?" Dahlia leaned forward. "Anything interesting happen?"

Bryony scanned the pages. "Not really. Waterloo Bridge still isn't open. Parliament is debating the reintroduction of the sovereign." She glanced up. "There was another Princess Caraboo sighting."

"Bah." Dahlia wrinkled her nose. "Who cares about foreign princesses when there are more pressing concerns closer to home?"

"Here's something." Bryony folded the paper to highlight a section of classified advertisements. "Look at this poor bastard."

"*Bryony Grenville*," Camellia admonished, while her sisters still believed her in possession of the moral high ground to do so. "A lady doesn't curse."

Dahlia let out a slow whistle. "She does when she reads *this*."

My darling Lady X,

You know who I am. I cannot claim the same. But I want to know you. I need to. You have stolen my heart. It is my fervent wish that you keep it, for I will be forever yours. Please meet me, if only for a moment.

I will be on Vauxhall Bridge at dusk. Wear your mask if you must. I won't turn around unless you grant me permission.

The stars simply aren't the same without you beneath them.

Yours ever,

W

"'*W*?'" Bryony exclaimed. "Who on earth could that be?"

"Wainwright," Camellia choked out before she could stop herself. Her heart pounded as she reread the words. It had to be him. It had to be for *her*. Light-headedness assailed her. There was no other explanation.

"Wainwright?" Dahlia repeated in disbelief. "*Lord* Wainwright? The heartless, emotionless rakehell?"

"Smitten with a mystery woman," Bryony crowed in glee. "The Lord of Pleasure himself. How rich! It's positively delicious."

"Positively," Camellia echoed, her throat suddenly dry. A desperate, humorless laugh bubbled within her. Lord Wainwright had written her a love letter.

How could he ever believe she would answer such a publication? How could she possibly keep herself from trying?

Bryony chortled in delight. "What woman would be powerful enough to bring down a prize stud like that?"

"I would love to meet her!" Dahlia agreed.

Hands trembling, Camellia refrained from participating in speculation. Her sisters would kill her if they found out the truth. Which of course they would, if she were to answer the advertisement.

After all, the earl had been recognized. There were witnesses to her ruin. Linking Camellia's name to such a scandalous affair would destroy the reputations of everyone in her family... and the trust of her sisters.

Dahlia would feel personally betrayed. Camellia's parents would be even more disappointed. She was the *good* girl. The one they could count upon to do as she was told. To stay out of trouble. To marry a stranger. To never say no.

And yet... She couldn't help but read the romantic words again and again. Could it possibly be true? Could Lord Wainwright mean even a fraction of what he had said?

"What time is it?" she asked as casually as she could.

Bryony glanced over Camellia's shoulder at the clock on the mantel. "Half seven. Why, have you an assignation?"

Half seven. The sun was already setting.

"I'm... late for a fitting with my modiste," Camellia lied and pushed to her feet. "For my... wedding."

The one that would never happen.

Dahlia set down her plate of biscuits and brushed the crumbs from her hands. "I'll go with you."

"No," Camellia said quickly, then blushed. "Not this time. It's..."

"Intimate apparel?" Bryony guessed with a flutter of her eyelashes. "I would love to have intimate apparel of my own."

"Not with Mr. Bost, you wouldn't," Dahlia muttered under her breath.

"I'm standing right here," Camellia reminded them, then slid her arms into her warmest pelisse. "And now I'm gone. Be good, please."

She slipped from the room before God could strike her down for hypocrisy.

By the time her hired hack reached Vauxhall

Bridge, the sun had disappeared. She stared out through the dusty window at the tall figure standing alone amidst the cast-iron arches.

Lord Wainwright. He was *here*. Staring out at the soot-stained horizon with an expression of utter despondency.

He must have been here for hours. Waiting for Lady X. Hoping she might see his paid advertisement. Praying she would answer his plea.

Camellia remained in the hackney, her hands shaking with uncertainty.

She could end this farce right here. But should she? What good could come of confronting him? Of divulging who she was? Explaining why she had never been available?

Would *he* even be interested if he knew she wasn't a mysterious lady in emerald silk, but mousy old Camellia Grenville, spinster sister to the hoyden and the termagant? No one would ever mistake her for a countess.

From the safety of her hackney prison, she watched him for the better part of an hour. He never strayed from his watch post against a stone pier. She gave the driver an extra shilling and pressed her face against the dirty glass.

Her heart twisted as an hour bled into the next. The earl stood handsome and stoic and utterly alone. Waiting for a woman who would never arrive... because she had never existed. Lady X was a fantasy. Wainwright lived in his world and Camellia in hers. The distinction was best for everyone.

When the night turned too dark to make out his outline, she gave the driver another shilling and bade him return home.

Tonight had been a mistake. Just like all the others.

She would not return.

CHAPTER 24

*D*espite the early sun streaming through Michael's study windows the following morning, the day didn't seem as bright as it had the week before. Nothing did. Though he tried to focus on the documents his man of business had delivered, his mind kept returning to Lady X.

She hadn't come. He'd stood alone on the iron bridge until even the waxing moon could no longer penetrate the sooty sky, and still she had not come.

Perhaps Lady X hadn't seen his advertisement. It was possible. But she knew his name. She didn't need an advertisement to know where to direct a letter or send a footman. If she wished to resume communication with him, she could.

But she did not.

Michael set his jaw. Somehow, he would have to go to her. He had been the one to botch the affair. He would have to be the one to fix things. But how?

He drummed his fingers atop the mahogany desk and stared at the bookshelves lining his office wall. Hawkridge! Didn't the marquess have a cousin or some such who was a Bow Street Runner? Mr... Spaulding, if Michael wasn't mistaken.

Perfect. He leapt to his feet. A chap like that would be well experienced in apprehension and investigation. Finding Lady X would be easy. Mr. Spaulding would have the matter sorted in no time at all.

Michael hurried to fetch a hat and coat. There would be plenty of time later for business, once he'd at least had the opportunity to address Lady X in person. It was the not knowing that had him so tied up in knots. The wondering, the wanting, the waiting. He just wished to speak with her. To explain he wanted her for her, and no other reason. To make her realize she possessed his heart.

If, after that, Lady X still wished nothing to do with him... well. As much as he would hurt, he respected her too much to force her to wed him if that was not what she wished. If *he* was not who she wished.

He loved her. He wanted to share a lifetime of happiness, not a loveless marriage rife with resentment.

All he could do was state his case. Try to convince her of his sincerity. Hope to win her affection, or at least an opportunity to court her properly. No masks, no subterfuge. Just a lovestruck earl with his heart on his sleeve.

When Michael's coach arrived at the Magistrates' Court at 4 Bow Street, the sight of the wide, three-story structure filled him with hope —and a much-needed sense of confidence. With luck, he would be able to pay a formal call on Lady X this very afternoon.

He strode through the front door and presented himself to a ruddy-cheeked fellow at the main desk. "Good morning. My name is Lord Wainwright. I am here to see Mr. Spaulding."

"I am Mr. Spaulding." A swarthy, dark-haired man with wide shoulders and a casual posture leaned against the doorway to a rear office. He did not glance up from the papers in his hands. "I do not know a Lord Wainwright, nor have we an appointment."

"True on both counts." Michael doffed his beaver hat with a smile. "Allow me to put you at ease. I am good friends with Lord Hawkridge—"

"Ah," Mr. Spaulding interrupted softly. "My half-brother. Now I am certainly at ease. Has your marquessate also misplaced its fortune?"

Taken aback, Michael narrowed his eyes at the Runner. Perhaps this was not the easiest path to success. "Earldom. And, no, I'm afraid my finances are fully in order."

"Then why are you here? Let me guess." Mr. Spaulding lifted his brows. "A woman?"

Michael gave a self-conscious cough behind his gloved fist. "Your powers of deduction are quite astute."

"Nonsense," the Runner said briskly. "Amongst my half-brother's set, the primary problems are lost money or insubordinate ladies. Is yours being too amorous or not amorous enough?"

"I'll thank you not to make light of my concerns," Michael said stiffly.

Mr. Spaulding returned his gaze to his papers. "I'll thank *you* not to waste my time."

Michael refrained from curling his fingers into fists. "If you don't wish to help people, why become a Runner?"

"I am not Cupid. I do not make love potions or settle wagers. I solve crimes." Mr. Spaulding made a point of glancing at his pocket watch. "Unless you've a theft or a murder to report, our business is concluded."

Michael felt the last vestiges of hope slipping away. "I'll pay."

"Still not interested." The Runner returned his gaze to his papers. "Adieu."

Of all the insolent, high-handed—Michael choked down his anger. Losing his temper would not solve any of his problems. "You..."

Mr. Spaulding gazed back at him blandly.

Michael forced his tight shoulders to relax. The Runner was right. Michael's situation with Lady X did not fall under the city's jurisdiction. There had, however, been a crime he had not previously thought to report. Since he was here, he supposed he ought to mention it.

"A few weeks ago, an item was stolen from my —" He shook his head. The harp necklace had been lost and found. What was the Runner meant

ERICA RIDLEY

to do about it now? "Never mind. I shan't waste any more of your time. Good day."

He turned toward the door.

"Wait." Mr. Spaulding stepped forward. "I presume you live in Mayfair?"

Slowly, Michael turned back toward the Runner. "I do."

"What was stolen?" Mr. Spaulding's posture was now one of interest.

Michael feared his small theft was about to disappoint. "A solid gold harp, slightly larger than a locket. It had been meant as a necklace bauble."

The Runner nodded. "Small enough to fit in the palm of one's hand?"

"Unquestionably." Michael frowned. These were not the crown jewels. Why so much interest in a memento that only mattered to one man?

Mr. Spaulding's focus did not waver. "Had it been kept under lock and key?"

"It had not." Nor could Michael forgive himself for that oversight. For failing to lock the door, he had only himself to blame.

The Runner's hard countenance eased. "Don't brood so. I am not in the habit of blaming victims for crimes perpetrated by villains. Particularly not where the slippery Thief of Mayfair is concerned."

Michael started in surprise. "I am not the first?"

"You are not the only case, but you might well be the first." Mr. Spaulding's gaze sharpened. "Three weeks ago, you said?"

Michael frowned. "Perhaps closer to four or five. I had hosted a soirée…"

"When did you recover the missing piece?"

He blinked. "How did you—"

"The crimes are identical," Mr. Spaulding explained. "A small but expensive item goes missing. Perhaps it was stolen. Perhaps it was misplaced. There had been a party, a new maid, a distraction. Within a week, the item is found at a pawnbroker. Never the same storefront twice. Never sold by the same person. Because the missing item has now been recovered, its owners rarely seek restitution. How close am I to your case?"

"Spot on," Michael admitted with grudging respect. "How did you determine there was a pattern, if no one reported the losses?"

"Slowly." The Runner rubbed his jaw. "But never fear. The Thief of Mayfair is a pest that will be squashed. Now that I have determined there *is* a case, I shall not rest until the perpetrator has been brought to justice."

"Mr. Spaulding is the cleverest investigator in all of London," the man at the front desk put in with pride. "'Tis only a matter of time before your thief meets the gallows."

At that news, Michael simply felt empty. The harp was back home. He didn't care about chasing a petty thief to the gallows. He cared about Lady X. He wished the cleverest investigator in London would spare a second to find *her.*

Despondency weighted his bones. Lady X's

presence was what was truly missing from Michael's home. At this rate, he would never find her. There was nothing left to try.

This time, when he turned toward the door, no one stopped him.

Michael climbed back into his carriage and stared at its luxurious, empty interior. He yearned for Lady X. What use were all his riches without the woman he most wished to share them with?

"Where to, milord?" asked the driver.

Where to, indeed. Michael let his head fall back against the carriage wall. Perhaps Lady X was lost to him forever, perhaps she was not. The only thing he knew for certain was that his whirling mind was in no condition to be making important decisions about his estate. He would return to the duties of his title tomorrow. Today, he could use a long walk to clear his head.

"Hyde Park," he commanded the driver.

The stately coach sprang into motion.

Once Michael was alone on a twisting path through the least-frequented acres, he allowed himself to forget his troubles for a moment and enjoy a solitary stroll amongst the calming beauty of nature.

With every rustle of leaves or trill of a robin, his step and heart grew lighter. The meeting with the Runner had not gone as Michael wished, but all was not lost. A single day had passed since last he saw Lady X. She knew his name. Perhaps she only needed time.

He frowned as he passed a break in the trail that led not to a pedestrian path, but rather to some shadowed section of untamed thicket. Strange. He had crossed through here once before. He remembered this curve in the road, and the fallen log wedged between the trees.

This was where the eldest Miss Grenville had burst upon him from out of nowhere, ruining a perfectly folded cravat by smashing her face into it, and then ruining a perfectly peaceful outing with false quotations about Michael's direct road to hell.

He paused and tried to peer through the trees. What the devil had the maddening woman been about? Why had she been alone—and so far from the manicured pedestrian trail near the front of the park?

Curiosity got the better of him. With a sigh, he stepped over the fallen log into a narrow gap amongst the thicket. Nettles snagged the tails of his coat and clung to the kerseymere of his breeches.

And then, just as suddenly... he was free.

A sunny patch of brilliantly green grass lined the shoulder of a crystal blue river. Beautiful trees with thick brown trunks and a profusion of fluttering leaves stretched overhead.

There were no trodden flowers, no bits of forgotten rubbish, no sign at all that anyone else had ever set foot in this idyllic retreat. Just the sweet scent of clean air, the gentle murmur of the sparkling stream, and an enormous gray rock with a wide, smooth surface perfect for lying back and simply being at peace.

Not *a* rock. *The* rock. Michael's heart thumped in shock. He had found Lady X's secret river spot. Here. In Hyde Park.

Good Lord. His jaw dropped in disbelief. Miss Grenville was Lady X.

Dumbfounded, he climbed atop the waist-high rock and dangled his feet above the rippling river, as she must have done a hundred times before. His head swam with dizziness at what was now obvious.

Miss Grenville was Lady X.

Thunderstruck, he stared at all the beauty around him. Recalled the words they'd exchanged on the path. The evenings they'd shared at the masquerade. The moment he'd told her he would be hers forever if only she would have him. The night he'd called her sister a termagant.

Of course she hadn't called. Miss Grenville had hated him long before the widow Epworth had stumbled upon the Lord of Pleasure relieving a masked woman of her maidenhead. Michael winced. Miss Grenville's well-deserved shock at the interruption hadn't been shame at being caught in the act of losing her virginity after all.

Her horror had come from discovering she'd done so with *him*.

Melancholy, he propped his elbows on his thighs and stared out over the water. No matter what she might believe, he had meant every word he'd spoken as Lord X. The moments they'd shared had been the most honest, most precious evenings of his life.

With her, he wasn't an earl or a rakehell or a caricature. With her, he'd been able to be himself. To be Michael. To fall in love.

Knowing her true identity didn't change any of that. If anything, his respect for her grew stronger. Their names may have been false, but their connection was real. Both as Miss Grenville and as Lady X, their interactions had been infused with a frankness rarely experienced.

When Miss Grenville was vexed with him, she did not hesitate to let him know. And when Lady X was pleased with him, when she wished him to stop talking and take her somewhere more private... But what could he do?

One word to her father and Miss Grenville would be forced to the altar. But that was the last thing Michael wished. One could not force one's suit upon a woman as independent as her.

He wanted her to choose him. Wanted her to decide on her own that they were better together than apart. Wanted her not as Lady X or as Miss Grenville, but as his countess. His wife. His equal. Michael slid from the rock and picked his way back to the main path. Hope dared to once again slip inside his heart.

It would not be easy, but their love was worth any risk.

CHAPTER 25

*T*he following morning, Camellia had the day's papers brought up with her breakfast tray.

In the event Wainwright had taken out another advertisement—or the scandal columnists had identified the fallen woman fleeing the masquerade—she much preferred not discovering the news in front of her sisters.

As she'd feared, the front page of the paper bore Lord Wainwright's name in bold type.

To her relief, however, the article had nothing to do with her. Or anything scandalous at all. The earl had apparently been instrumental in the committee responsible for a reintroduction of the gold sovereign, this time bearing a laureate profile on one side and the slaying of a dragon on the other. According to the article, the Latin motto of the Order of the Garter was embossed along the outer edge.

Impressed, she touched her fingers to the artist's rendering. The new coins sounded stunning. She could scarcely wait to see one in person.

She flipped through the rest of the pages, scanning for any other mention of Lord Wainwright's name—or hers. She paused at the top of the paid advertisements.

The Cloven Hoof
hereby announces
Lord Wainwright has won
his forty-day wager

Wryly, Camellia wondered if anyone had dared to take that wager, or if Lord Wainwright himself would be the sole recipient of the winnings.

She bit her lip. Forty days ago, she would have been one of the first in line to bet against him. Like the others, she would have been wrong. Guilt pricked at her. She had judged him far more harshly than he had deserved.

Her shoulders slumped at the unflattering realization. She had accepted society's image of him without questioning. The image that he himself helped portray, just as she did when she pretended to be a mouse with no will of her own. Perhaps forty days ago, she could be forgiven for accepting false assumptions as the only possible truth.

But now she knew better. She knew *him*. He was so much more than the rakehell he'd been painted. Now that the wager was over and he was free to do whatever he wished, he *was* doing what he wished. His preference wasn't seducing debutantes. He was leading committees in the House of Lords. Managing his earldom. Enjoying London. Penning love letters.

In fact, for the past several weeks, the only times Camellia had ever witnessed him flirting with anyone…

It had been with her.

She caught her breath. Her traitorous heart beat faster at the memories. The heat of his kisses. Their waltz beneath the stars. The pleasure they had found together when—

Heat flooded her cheeks. Quickly, she flipped to the next page in the paper. The center advertisement immediately caught her eye.

My darling Lady X,

I found the place we dreamed of. The rock is everything you promised. All it lacks is you. I'll be there every day at noon until you meet me. I miss you. I long to hear your voice.

If you don't wish to come for me, then come for your earring. If you do not, I am likely to cherish it forever.

Yours always,
W

CAMELLIA CLOSED the paper with shaking fingers, then reopened it to the same page and reread the advertisement a dozen more times.

It was him. Missing her. Just as dreadfully as she yearned for him. But the future he promised was not meant to be.

They were star-crossed. An earl could never accept a mere Grenville as his countess. Phineas Mapleton had said so at the circus. But Camellia had known long before that. Earls took women of lesser standing as mistresses, not wives. And she had no wish to be his temporary mistress.

A girl like her considered herself fortunate when she received an offer from a gentleman like Mr. Bost. Twice her age, perhaps, but a solid match whose standing would not reflect badly on her younger sisters.

Although Lord Wainwright's rakehell reputation may have been exaggerated out of proportion, any connection would still be scandalous by association. He must realize. Even if the earl were willing to make an honest woman of her now that she'd been ruined, doing so would jeopardize the reputations of her younger sisters.

The moment they appeared publicly, the troublemaking Mrs. Epworth would realize Camellia had been the disheveled young lady in Lord Wainwright's bed. One anonymous word and gossip would fly. Camellia would be known not as a countess, but as an easy conquest. Speculation would run high that her sisters were cut from the same cloth.

And yet… she could not let him keep waiting by the river in the hopes his Lady X would arrive. They might have no future together, but the heartfelt moments they'd shared in the past had meant as much to Camellia as they seemed to mean to the earl.

He deserved an answer. Even if it was one he would not like.

After breakfast, she dressed with the same care she'd given her appearance on the nights of the masquerades. Her lips twisted with self-deprecation as she turned away from the looking-glass. This time, she would not be Lady X, but Miss Camellia Grenville. She was bound to disappoint.

The hack dropped her at a side entrance to the park at half past eleven. Pulse pounding alarmingly, she made her way from the path, to the trail, to the thicket, to the river.

He was there.

Her heart skipped at the sight.

He was seated atop the big gray rock, gazing at the river. His back was to her. Although she approached softly, his spine straightened as if he sensed her nearness.

"Lady X?" he asked quietly without turning to face her.

Her answering smile was bittersweet. She was glad he could not see it. "It is me."

"Would you like me to turn around?"

Would she? Camellia hesitated. "Perhaps it is best if you do not."

He inclined his head as if he had anticipated her reply, then gestured toward a small package at the base of the rock. "Your earring."

She bent to scoop up a parcel wrapped in brown paper. It was too large to merely be her lost earring. The box nearly spanned the width of two palms.

"Lord X..."

"Open it."

She tugged at the bow to unwrap the string. The paper fell loose as well. Carefully, she lifted the lid of the wide, flat box.

Inside was her missing earring. And a matching necklace made not of cut glass, but teardrop shaped emeralds with matching diamonds.

"Wainwright," she gasped, her heart hammering at the thought of wearing such beautiful jewelry. "I cannot accept this."

"It is a gift." His tone was wry. "Surely you've no wish to offend my tender sensibilities. Men are remarkably fragile creatures."

"I'm not who you think I am," she stammered.

"Is anyone?" he asked softly. Even without being able to see his face, sunlight bathed him in a warm glow, making him seem larger than life. "I'd like to know you. I'd like your permission to call on you formally."

So would she, more than anything. Camellia forced herself to be strong. "I'm afraid that's out of the question."

"Then something less formal," he suggested quickly. "Vauxhall Gardens. Piccadilly Square. A stroll somewhere public so we won't be tempted to tear each other's clothing off."

She grinned despite herself. "Who says I'm tempted?"

"Aren't you?" His words were light, but his voice was defeated. "Was our time together not as meaningful for you as it was for me?"

Silence stretched between them as she fought for words she could say.

"It was temporary," she managed through the stinging in her throat.

"It doesn't have to be." He hunched his shoulders, then straightened. "Say you'll meet me face-to-face. Not as clandestine lovers, but at least as friends. Perhaps tonight?"

She bit her lip. "I cannot."

"Tomorrow night?" he asked quietly.

"I can't. I am… expected at a Grenville musicale." Perhaps the biggest understatement of all time.

"I'm afraid I won't be attending the show," he said, his tone more sad than droll. "I am not welcome in the Grenville household. I don't suppose

I can talk you into coming away with me instead?"

"I cannot." She took a deep breath. It was past time he knew the truth. "I'll be on stage."

When he turned around to face her, his countenance held a crooked smile rather than an expression of surprise. "I would love to hear you sing."

He *knew*.

She stared back at him, light-headed with shock. "How long have you known?"

"Since I found this paradise." He gestured at the lush beauty about them. "And recalled it was not Lady X, but Miss Grenville whom I had crossed paths with not ten yards away."

Camellia grimaced drily. She could only imagine the shock on his face when he realized he'd fallen for none other than mousy Miss Grenville, even for a whirlwind candlelit moment. "And you still wished to meet me?"

"I want a lot more than that." He slid down from the rock. "Did you not see my advertisements?"

She took a step in retreat. "I won't be your mistress."

He choked in horror. "I'm not asking you to be my mistr—"

"And I won't be your wife," she finished firmly. For his sake. For her sake. For her sisters' sakes.

His soulful green-brown-gray eyes gazed back at her, hurt.

She glanced away, unable to speak.

"May I ask why?" he asked.

"You might have won your wager," she said when she had regained her voice, "but you lost your reputation long before. Any romantic association with you brings gossip and scandal my family can ill afford. I am sorry."

"No," he said, his beautiful eyes full of regret. "*I* am sorry. The fault is mine."

He was trying to do the right thing, she realized. He had taken her virginity. For a gentleman, such an act required a trip to the altar.

But she didn't want him to fall upon his sword for her. She didn't want anyone to marry her just because it was the "proper thing" to do.

Especially not in this case, when it would all go so wrong. Instead of saving her reputation, he would tarnish two more in the process.

Bryony and Dahlia would never find husbands once the caricaturists printed etchings of their sister fleeing the bed of the Lord of Pleasure.

Camellia's chest ached with sadness and frustration. With their masks on, she and Lord Wainwright could be themselves. But without them... they could not have each other at all.

She removed her lost earring from the jewelry box and placed the lid back atop the necklace. "Here."

He shook his head. "It's yours."

She tied the brown paper around the parcel and nestled it back beside the rock.

"Thank you for the gesture," she said quietly. "And the memories."

Without giving him a chance to say anything that might make her foolish heart change its mind, she strode out of the hidden clearing and onto the path that led back to her real life.

Lord X was the dream she would have to leave behind.

CHAPTER 26

As she climbed into the first available hackney, Camellia's heart still pounded at the dizzying exchange she had just shared with Lord Wainwright. She had not meant to disclose her uninspiring identity, but she was glad she had done so.

He'd already known.

She swallowed. For Lord Wainwright, it hadn't changed a thing. For her, Lord X's true identity was a bigger stumbling block than she had even feared. She had taken an enormous risk just to say goodbye in person.

Her chest tightened with worry. She cast her gaze out the dirty glass of the hack window at the congested city streets. She had escaped the scandal columns the night of her ruin. That had been miracle enough. What if she had been seen with Lord Wainwright in the park? What if he told someone the truth, or an observant passer-by managed to put it together?

What if, in her attempt to save her sisters' reputations, she'd ruined them in the process?

Her fingers went cold. The moment the hired hack slowed in front of the Grenville townhouse, she leapt out and hurried through the front door and up the wooden staircase before her sisters could hear the gossip from someone else.

Both Bryony and Dahlia glanced up with identical startled faces when Camellia burst into their shared sitting room.

"I have a confession." Her heart thudded so loudly, she could scarce hear her own pronouncement. "I won't be marrying Mr. Bost."

"Thank *God*." Dahlia tossed a sheaf of papers aside in relief. "We can stop plotting how to kidnap you from Northumberland."

Camellia was too nervous to take a seat, but forced herself to perch on the edge of the chaise longue across from Bryony. They should all be sitting down for the rest of her confession.

"I cannot wed anyone," she forced herself to admit, "because I am ruined."

"You're *what?*" Bryony set down her violin with shaking fingers. "Who is this despicable cad who isn't gentleman enough to offer for you?"

"He offered," Camellia said quickly. "I said no."

"You what?" Dahlia squeaked, her face a mask of horror. "You're in no position to say no. Why would you do such a foolish thing?"

"That wasn't the foolish bit." Camellia took a deep breath. There was no going back. "The foolish part was… Lord Wainwright."

Both sisters stared back at her in shock for a long wordless moment.

"I didn't mean to. I promise," she assured them, her face aflame. "We were both wearing masks and had no idea who we were with until it was too late."

Her sisters' jaws dropped in tandem.

Camellia's cheeks burned. "I didn't know. And I realize that makes me sound like a brazen roundheels. Masks on, gown off. I'm afraid it was… exactly like it sounds. The tension had been building for weeks. By the time an opportunity presented itself…" She cleared her throat. "If it helps at all, I believe Lord Wainwright was just as shocked to learn my identity as I was his."

Both sisters blinked.

The first to regain her senses was Bryony, who tumbled off her fainting couch in peals of laughter.

Dahlia, however, did not join in the giggles. She stared at her elder sister as if Camellia had sprouted hooves and a tail.

"I'm sorry." Camellia lowered her gaze. "I know you said you'd never forgive us if we so much as spoke to him. This is infinitely worse."

"Infinitely better," Bryony corrected, propping herself up off the floor. "What Dahlia said was that she wanted to take him down a peg. I'd say making him fall in love with you only to cut him from your life easily counts."

Camellia's heart raced faster. "He's not in *love*

with me. He's an earl. A gentleman. He offered to marry me because he wished to do the right thing."

Dahlia pursed her lips. "Wainwright may be an earl, but he's no gentleman."

"Deliciously not," Bryony agreed, pretending to fan herself with her gloved hand. "You just said he didn't know who you were. There was no *need* to be a gentleman. How ruined are you? If you made love to him at the masquerade—"

"I might have," Camellia admitted, her voice strangled.

"—then there was certainly no expectation of proper behavior on anyone's part." Bryony's eyes sparkled. "Wainwright has money, a title, good looks… He has never done a single thing he didn't wish to do. If he asked you to marry him, he meant it."

"Did you say 'no' because you meant it?" Dahlia asked quietly.

"I…" Camellia's neck heated. "I may have said 'no' because we were caught."

"Caught!" Bryony crowed in delight. "Why haven't we heard rumor of the scandal?"

"Wainwright was recognized, but I was not. For now," Camellia added with a wince. "If I align myself with him publicly, it won't take the gossip columnists more than a single afternoon to determine that I was the mysterious lady in the earl's bed."

"It sounds delightfully sordid," Bryony said in

a hushed whisper. "I am impressed. Why don't I ever get to do anything sordid?"

"You're not trying hard enough," Dahlia informed her sternly. "If Cam can bring the most infamous rakehell in London up to scratch, I shall be mortified if my baby sister can't muster up a moment or two of scandal."

Camellia's mouth fell open. "You're not angry? Either of you?"

"There's nothing *you* need to apologize for," Dahlia hedged. "I've forgiven the earl."

Camellia and Bryony exchanged a suspicious glance. Dahlia not holding a grudge might sound positive, but was more likely to be a terrible omen. She had been known only to forgive after exacting revenge. Their brother's left foot was still dyed purple.

"So you're even?" Bryony pressed, narrowing her eyes at Dahlia. "Cam can have as torrid an affair with Lord Wainwright as she pleases?"

She frowned in surprise. "Cam doesn't need *my* permission for a torrid affair. She shouldn't require anyone's permission for anything." Dahlia swung her wide-eyed gaze toward her elder sister. "Cam, when are you ever going to start doing what *you* want?"

Camellia had tried that. It hadn't worked. She gave a weak smile. "I'm the elder sister. It has never mattered what I want. Only what's best for the family."

"Of course it matters," Bryony exclaimed. "That delicious man is in love with you!"

"He's in love with Lady X," Camellia corrected. "She never existed. Only plain old Camellia Grenville exists."

"And what does plain old Camellia Grenville want?" Dahlia asked softly. "Spinsterhood? Northumberland?"

"The opera," Camellia said softly. "Ever since I was a child, what I wanted most was to sing professionally. I knew I couldn't have it, of course. A daughter in theater would ruin the entire family." She laughed humorlessly. "So I fell in love with a rakehell instead."

Bryony's eyes sparkled. "If you want to sing opera and marry Wainwright, then you absolutely should."

"I agree." Dahlia leaned forward. "I'm pursuing *my* dream of helping London's indigent girls find their feet. Heaven knows Bryony does whatever she wants."

Bryony nodded earnestly. "Quite true. I've been rather worse than usual of late."

"If the worst scandal you can imagine is taking advantage of your incredible voice and marrying the man you love…" Dahlia looped her arm about Camellia's shoulders and pulled her into a warm hug. "I would never forgive myself for standing in your way."

"It wouldn't be my scandal alone," Camellia stammered, hugging her sister back for all she was worth. "Your reputations would be ruined by association. The gossips will assume all three of us are fallen women."

ERICA RIDLEY

"Let them." Bryony shrugged defiantly. "It was only a matter of time until I managed to ruin my reputation on my own. Your future happiness is a far better reason to get started."

"I'm headmistress of a school for wayward girls," Dahlia pointed out. "Not a convent. The only souls who believe me an angel are my students. I certainly cannot expect my own sister to be. In fact, I would be delighted to inform Mr. Bost that you must regretfully decline to wed yourself to a stranger."

"Beast!" Bryony whacked Dahlia's shoulder. "I shall be utterly disconsolate if *I* am not the one chosen to impart the marvelous news."

"Then I must disappoint both of you wretched creatures," Camellia said with a choking laugh. "Mr. Bost may not have chosen me for love, but he does not deserve to be treated shabbily. I shall pen him a letter at once, so that he does not waste a four-day trip."

"And *we*," Dahlia said softly, "are delighted beyond measure that you will not be wasting the rest of your life. You have too much talent and too big a heart not to use them both to their fullest potential."

Throat stinging, Camellia embraced her sisters and did her best not to cry in their hair. There wasn't anything she wouldn't do for them —or they for her. She loved them more than anything on this earth.

The most precious wedding present her sisters had given her wasn't their well-wishes or the exotic gowns they'd commissioned for her to wear to the masquerade.

It was the freedom to decide her future for herself.

CHAPTER 27

*M*ichael leaned against the cold brick of his fireplace. With unseeing eyes, he sifted idly through a stack of correspondence. So many cards, letters, invitations. And yet the only person whose voice he longed to hear never wished to speak to him again.

Despondent, he glanced over at the table, where yesterday's paper yet lay. Michael still wasn't certain whether to frame the Cloven Hoof's announcement or to burn it.

Despite all odds, he had won the forty day wager—but the victory could not have felt more hollow. He felt no relief over what he had won because all he could think about was who he had lost. And how much she meant.

Camellia had said that winning hadn't changed anything. That his reputation was still too scandalous to take his proposal seriously. Yet Michael had never been more serious about anything in his life.

There were plenty of other women who would have valued a countess's life of luxury over something so ephemeral as a reputation. The silver tray on his mantel overflowed with calling cards of ladies hoping to ensnare an earl by any means necessary.

He didn't want just any woman. He wanted the one he loved. The one he had hoped to share his life with, not merely share a title. Without Camellia, the rest didn't matter. No amount of riches could bring joy to a loveless marriage.

And she was right. He'd won a wager, not a war. The battle to improve his reputation in society's eyes was far from over. It might take months, years, before London thought of him as the Earl of Wainwright rather than the Lord of Pleasure.

But he didn't have years to work on improving his image before winning Camellia back. He might not even have months. Some other toff —a *true* gentleman—would already have swept her off her feet and whisked her to the nearest altar. If Michael wanted an opportunity to change her mind, he needed to make his case before it was too late. But how, if she refused to even speak to him?

He snapped his gaze back to the stacks of calling cards and correspondence upon the mantel. A spark of hope sizzled across his skin. Camellia may not wish to resume their conversation, but if he wanted to hear her voice... perhaps he still could.

An electric excitement ran through his veins as he rifled through the piles of unopened correspondence until he found the only invitation that mattered. The Grenville soirée musicale. Tonight. No—not just tonight. *Right now.*

He shoved the small rectangle into the inner pocket of his greatcoat and strode straight to the mews. There was no time to waste with summoning a servant to ready the horses or coaxing his refined coachman into driving with more urgency than befitted an earl.

There wasn't a moment to spare. Michael would drive himself in his swiftest phaeton.

If he arrived after the performance had begun, he would not be granted entry. Indeed, even though the invitation was hand-lettered to him by Lady Grenville herself, he still had to cross the threshold. If the butler remembered him as the man Camellia had thrown out and instructed never to return…

Oh, who was Michael fooling? Of *course* the butler would recall such a memorable incident. Michael's first task wasn't winning a private word with Camellia. It was wheedling his way through the front door.

Reins in hand, he raced his phaeton through Mayfair's cobblestone streets. When he arrived at the Grenville townhouse, he handed over the carriage and a gold sovereign to the closest footman and strode up the walk to the front door.

The butler's lips pursed in distaste upon sight.

Michael's hopes fell. No matter. He would fall to his knees and beg if necessary. "My name is—"

"Lord Wainwright," the butler finished darkly. He stepped forward as if to block the entrance. Although he had quickly schooled his features into the carefully blank expression worn by front door staff, the butler showed no sign of stepping aside to grant the earl entry. As trusted staff, he likely considered the girls to be under his protection... and had no intention of allowing them to be hurt anew. "Is the family expecting you?"

Michael rather doubted it. He fumbled for the invitation in his greatcoat pocket and presented the side bearing his name with a flourish. "I am in possession of a personal invitation for tonight's musicale."

"I see." The butler did not move.

Michael's gut filled with dread. "Has it already begun?"

"It has not," the butler replied slowly. "Although I expect it shall at any moment."

There was still time! Michael tried not to display his frustration. "Then may I please come in and take my seat?"

"It's standing room only." The butler's scowl faded. He sighed and stepped aside. "But you may try."

The acquiescence was so unexpected, Michael blinked twice before he realized the butler was indeed allowing him to cross the threshold. Renewed hope stretched his face into a grin. "I... I may come inside?"

"Miss Bryony and Miss Dahlia both gave me explicit orders," the butler responded stiffly.

But not Camellia. Michael's smile dimmed. At least he had been granted entrance. It was more than expected. What happened next was up to him.

He thanked the butler and followed a footman to an open door leading to the rear of a well-appointed salon. Michael's head jerked back in surprise at the scene inside.

Standing room only didn't begin to describe the astonishing crush of people present. He stared in disbelief. He'd had no idea the Grenville musicales were this popular. In fact, he'd heard that the same siblings presented the same score in the same format year after year. Yet there were almost as many bodies crammed into one small townhouse as there were attendees at Lambley's sprawling masquerades.

"The performance is about to begin," prompted the footman. "All doors must be closed to preserve acoustical purity."

"Of course," Michael stammered, and stepped into the room as the door followed right behind him.

Rows of chairs filled the room in two large blocks. Those who had not arrived early enough to secure a seat stood shoulder-to-shoulder about the perimeter. Every eye focused on the small wooden stage at the front of the room. A pianoforte stood to one side, and a thick velvet curtain on the other.

Despite the incredible number of guests in attendance, the salon was completely hushed. The air fairly crackled with excitement and anticipation.

Michael eased along the crowd until he found a bare scrap of wainscoting to lean against by the far wall. It was much farther from the stage than he would have liked, and not at all the best angle to view a performance, but by the looks of things he was fortunate to have found a spot to stand at all.

Lady Grenville stepped out from behind a curtain to the side of the stage and strode to the center to face her guests. "Thank you all for coming to share a night of magic and music. If this is your first time joining us, please allow me to introduce my children as they take the stage. First, my only son: Mr. Heath Grenville."

A handsome young man with a secretive smile strode out from behind the curtain.

No one clapped. No one even moved. Yet the excitement in the room was even more palpable than before.

The show was finally going to start.

"Mother. Guests." Mr. Grenville bowed to the hushed room and took a seat at the pianoforte.

Lady Grenville beamed at her son, then turned back to the crowd. "Next, my eldest daughter: Miss Camellia Grenville."

Michael snapped to attention as Camellia stepped out from behind the curtain in a simple, butter-yellow evening dress. His heart tripped. It was nothing like the elaborate bejeweled gowns paired with exotic feather masks she had worn to the masquerades, and yet she had never looked more lovely to him than she did tonight.

No amount of diamonds and plumes could compare to the beauty of seeing her actual face. Michael would happily spend the rest of his life with both of them in rags if it meant there would be no more masks keeping them apart.

"And last," Lady Grenville continued with obvious pride. "My youngest daughter: Miss Bryony Grenville."

When the youngest chit stepped out with a violin in hand, Michael barely managed to restrain a gasp of shock. Because he'd spent the last decade-and-a-half haunting music stores across the continent in search of unique harps, he recognized the instrument for what it was.

Bryony Grenville's violin was a work of art. A musical masterpiece crafted by none other than the famed luthier Antonio Stradivari. What on earth was happening?

Lady Grenville took her seat in the front row next to her husband.

Michael stood a little straighter. He'd always known that the Grenvilles were neither rich nor poor, neither shunned nor especially fashionable. He'd believed their much-publicized musicales to be nothing more than a mother's obvious attempt to draw a level of attention to her daughters that they might not otherwise receive. Three suitors for three daughters was too important a task to be left to Almack's alone.

But the middle daughter wasn't even present. The youngest had a *Stradivarius* that cost as much as the townhouse they lived in. It was the son who sat at the pianoforte. And Camellia...

What had Hawkridge said, that day at the circus? The marquess had claimed Camellia's voice was far superior to the current reigning soprano —a woman internationally famous for the beauty of her voice.

Lady Pettibone had immediately censured the idea of a proper young woman throwing her life and reputation away on something as vulgar as the theater, and the conversation had taken a sharply different path.

Heath Grenville arranged his fingers on the pianoforte and began to play. When Bryony Grenville touched her bow to her strings, Michael's breath caught from the exquisite sweetness of the sound.

And then Camellia opened her mouth to sing.

The rest of the world fell away. All Michael could feel was the enraptured thump of his heart. All he could see was Camellia's expressive face. And then not even that. Her voice filled the room, filled his body, filled his head and his heart and his soul.

He was no longer standing in a claustrophobic salon with four inches of wainscoting protruding into his back, but transported to another world.

To the vast, endless sky. The joyful notes were like shooting stars exploding across the heavens. The sorrowful chorus ripped his heart from his chest.

The Grenvilles didn't merely play music. They forced their guests to feel it, to live it, to *be* it.

Heath Grenville was more talented than Michael had ever suspected. Bryony Grenville was nothing short of phenomenal. But *Camellia...* Her voice was capable of lifting people out of themselves and into the music itself. Every word was a painting, every soaring trill an adventure.

Michael had never been more in awe—or more in love. She was incredible.

Only when the song ended and her brother began playing the introduction to the next did Michael become aware of murmurs rippling through the room.

He turned to the person next to him. "What is it? What's happening?"

"I don't know," replied a wide-eyed gentleman. "This is the sixth song, not the second song. They've never strayed from the score."

Michael frowned. "I'm not sure a change in the order counts as straying from the score."

"*Shh!*" A man to the other side waved Michael to silence without taking his gaze from the stage. "Hush. Something must be happening."

Michael fell silent. Not because the other gentleman had asked him to, but because Camellia had once again started to sing.

She turned words into emotions, lyrics into reality. Her voice ran through his veins like lifeblood, filling him with joy, then despair, then hope, then love. She held the entire room in thrall as she lifted her audience up and tossed them down with the magic of her voice. Not a single person breathed until the song was over.

Dazed, Michael turned to the man next to him in wonder. "Is it always like this?"

The gentleman blinked slowly, as if coming to after a sultry evening in an opium den.

"Always," he whispered. "Although tonight is even better than—"

Every guest froze in obvious shock as Heath Grenville began to play the next song.

"What is it?" Michael glanced around in alarm. "What's happening?"

"It's…a new song," came the disbelieving voice of a gentleman on the other side. "It's *never* a new song."

Camellia stepped up to the edge of the stage to face the audience.

"Tonight, I am going to sing an aria currently being performed at the Theatre Royal in Covent Garden." She took a deep breath and smiled at the crowd. "With luck, the next time I perform, it will be on that stage."

A collective gasp ran through the crowd.

Michael's heart stopped. He hadn't arrived here tonight just in time to hear her sing. He was watching her give up her reputation, her standing, and her future in order to pursue the thing she wanted most: performing live in an opera.

The sound of a hundred mouths falling open

in unison disappeared as the music swelled and Camellia once again began to sing. The notes dove and soared, the lyrics transporting the audience from the impotent rage of betrayal to the tender hope of love, of trust, of possibility.

He almost laughed when he realized the truth. He had come here tonight prepared to promise forty scandal-free years, not mere days, if that was what it took to win a second chance… and it turned out he wasn't the scandalous one after all.

Camellia was.

For Michael, it changed nothing. But he would never be able to forgive himself if he didn't encourage the love of his life to live her dream.

She wanted to be an opera singer? With a voice like that, the entire *world* needed her to be an opera singer.

If she were willing to accept him, he'd be more than happy to play second fiddle to a far more scandalous wife. But if the siren call of the theater filled her world so completely that there was no room left for Michael…

He swallowed his sorrow. Then he would have to let her go.

CHAPTER 28

*C*amellia ended her final note with more trepidation than she'd ever felt in her life. She'd announced her intent to pursue a career in theater to the entire ton, then promptly performed a scandalous piece from *Don Juan: A Grand Opera in Two Acts.*

Three songs in, and the musicale was over.

From this moment forward, Camellia was no longer a respectable woman. She was a future opera singer. Or at least she'd die trying.

She might become the most famous performer in England, or she might never rise from the obscurity of the chorus. Either way, her life as a proper young lady was over. Most of the people present tonight would never be able to share a roof with her again, unless it was from the safe distance of a theater box.

Once the shock settled, a few brave souls burst into spontaneous applause. Several others stood up and left the room. The rest stayed perfectly still to see what would happen next.

Camellia had no idea what was going to happen next. She didn't even know if she would remain welcome in her own home. Her siblings supported her one hundred percent, but Mother had very strong ideas about how she expected her daughters to live the rest of their lives.

Well, so did Camellia. Life was too short to spend it without the things one loved most.

She might not get to have it all, but at least she would have the opera.

Mother sprang to her feet and roared at the crowd. "Everybody go home! The musicale is over. Out! Out!"

Camellia stepped back into the wings.

Under normal circumstances, her mother screeching *Go home!* at the most fashionable, powerful people in the beau monde would have caused an even bigger scandal than Camellia had done with her announcement.

But these were not normal circumstances. Far from being offended, the audience members were delighted to escape into their carriages and parlors and dinner parties to gossip about what they'd just witnessed here tonight.

No one would remember Camellia's father looking at her as if he'd truly noticed her for the first time. No one would notice the nod of acceptance he gave her before escorting his shocked wife behind the curtain and off to their private chambers.

No one would recall the tall, golden-haired earl fighting his way upstream against the departing crowd to where Camellia now stood in the shadows.

"Wainwright." She forwent the traditional curtsy and forced herself to hold her ground. "Did you enjoy the show?"

"I wish it were longer," he said immediately, surprising her with his ferventness. "I wish I'd attended every musicale your family had ever performed. I wish I could hide in the chandeliers every time you open your mouth to sing, even when you aren't on stage."

Her cheeks heated in pleasure. "You *did* enjoy the show."

He took her hand. "You must know that your talent is incredible. I don't think you'll find work at the theater. I think you'll find fame."

The pleasure faded. No one knew actresses better than the Lord of Pleasure. Now that she had announced her disreputable plans to the world, what could he possibly want with her?

Camellia's voice was bleak. "Is that why you're here? To arrange a torrid affair with an opera singer instead of the usual actresses?"

"Nothing of the sort." His eyes were beseeching. "I don't want a torrid affair."

She hesitated. "You don't?"

"I want a torrid lifetime." He pressed her hands to his chest. "I want to do things with you that would make the walls blush. I want to fall asleep every night with you in my arms and the scent of your hair against my cheek. Even when we're old and wrinkled." He appeared to reconsider his words. "*Especially* when we're old and wrinkled."

She stared back at him, heart thudding with hope. "What are you saying?"

"I'm saying I don't love Lady X. I never did. I never will." His voice turned serious, his gaze intense. "I love Camellia Grenville. With or without a mask, my heart belongs to *you*."

Her breath caught as she stared back at him wordlessly.

"Despite everything that has happened, despite the chance that doing so may cause even more scandal—I still selfishly, utterly, desperately want you to marry me." He fell to one knee and placed her palm against his jaw. "Won't you make me the happiest of men?"

Camellia took a deep breath. Of course that was what she wanted. But he had to want it, too.

She touched his cheek. "Becoming an opera singer will drop me to the same social level as an actress, if my actions tonight haven't already done so."

He grasped her hands to his heart. "You want to be an opera singer? Be an opera singer. But please say you'll also be my wife."

"You won't be the Lord of Pleasure anymore," she warned him. "Not with a theater wife. You'll be a laughingstock."

"I'll be envied by all," he promised. "My

countess will be the most famous singer in England."

"Perhaps not for the right reasons," she said, her tone self-mocking. "Pursuing a career in opera has always been my dream, not a foregone conclusion. I may get laughed off the stage."

"Or you may find your name on every playbill from London to Rome." He smiled, then corrected himself. "*Our* name, that is. Lady Wainwright. Countess by day, soprano by night. I could get used to that."

"Don't expect me to sing *all* night," she demurred, arching a suggestive brow. "A countess also has certain duties which she must not neglect."

He stood up and pulled her into his arms with an arrogant grin. "Is that a 'yes,' Lady X?"

She twined her arms about his neck and kissed him with the promise of a thousand tomorrows. "Yes, Lord X. I would love to be your wife... because I love *you*."

CHAPTER 29

*M*ichael leaned against the sunny strip of wall between two of the harp room windows and grinned at his beautiful wife. Indescribable joy filled him at having her in his home. *Their* home. For the first time in well over a decade, the harp room was once again alive with music.

The cherubs smiling down at them from the brightly frescoed ceiling were no longer melancholy reminders of the past, but a promise of a long, happy future. He and Camellia had been wed for less than a day, and already Michael was more content than he could ever recall.

Speculation on whether his new wife was also the mystery lady who had fled his embrace at the masquerade had paled next to society's giddiness that the Lord of Pleasure had been brought to heel by none other than mousy Miss Grenville. Not that they were calling her "mousy" anymore!

Ever since the scandalous splash she'd made

singing the soaring lyrics of Don Juan's spurned lover at her family musicale, talk was not over whether Lady Wainwright had once attended a masquerade, but whether she would be taking the stage to perform Mozart's masterpiece live and without a mask.

The entire city planned to purchase tickets to witness a countess take part in theater.

The caricaturists were beside themselves with glee over the change in direction. Michael was no longer sketched as the Don Juan of England, but rather as a shamelessly smitten husband who fell to his wife's feet to listen to her sing.

Not far from the truth at all.

Michael grinned to himself as his green-eyed siren sang and hummed her way about the infamous harp room. Now that he was happily married, he wondered if society would finally cease to believe the music room a den of bacchanalia and iniquity... or if they assumed he and his wife kept the spirit of wickedness alive on their own.

They wouldn't be wrong.

Camellia spun to face him, her fingers tracing the mahogany curve of a shoulder-high harp. "It's a shame these beautiful instruments go unused."

He inclined his head. "I've thought the same thing for some time."

She lifted her fingers from the harmonic arch and came closer to toy with his cravat instead. "If you learn to play, I shall accompany you, and we can have our own musicales."

He captured her teasing lips in a kiss. "Private musicales?"

"Naked, private musicales," she promised as she led him to the window seat by his cravat. She climbed into his lap and twined her arms about his neck. "Isn't that what the harp room is for?"

"It is now," he growled as he claimed her mouth in a heated kiss.

For the rest of the night, the only music they made was their own.

EPILOGUE

*T*wo blissful years later, Camellia beamed at the packed, motley audience of the first annual Wainwright family musicale.

The entire Grenville clan was in attendance, as were the tenors, baritones, sopranos, and sundry crew who joined Camellia on stage for their command performances of *The Marriage of Figaro* at Covent Garden.

Neither Lady Jersey nor Lady Pettibone was in attendance, but it was hard to tell who else might be missing amongst the noisy, elbow-to-elbow crowd.

Camellia rescued her baby from the coddling arms of his favorite aunt, so that Bryony could join them on stage with her violin.

After settling one-year-old Henry on her hip, Camellia glanced over her shoulder at her husband. "Ready?"

It was all she could do not to burst into giggles at the pained look on his handsome face.

Of course he was not ready. Michael had no idea what to do with the harp-lute in his arms. But that was his own fault, since he had promised to learn it in time for their first family musicale.

Bryony's bow struck a high, clear note.

Camellia began to sing.

To the more discerning in the audience, her performance might not be quite on the same level as it had been during last season's run of *The Barber of Seville*.

But the discordant *plink, plink, plink* of her husband's red-and-blue stringed harp-lute punctuated by the high pitched "Ooh! Ooh!" of the ecstatic infant bouncing on her hip definitely made this the most memorable performance of Camellia's career.

Half the audience was in tears of laughter, clapping in a syncopated rhythm even worse than Michael's harp. The other half of the audience was on their feet, turning the rear of the parlor into a whirling, impromptu dance floor.

Whatever etchings tomorrow's caricaturists made of the fun-filled pandemonium here tonight, Camellia planned to frame every last one and put them in the harp room in a place of honor. Her life had turned out better than she had dreamed.

There was nowhere she'd rather be than surrounded by her favorite people, side by side with the man she loved.

THE END

THANK YOU FOR READING

Love talking books with fellow readers?

Join the *Historical Romance Book Club* for prizes, books, and live chats with your favorite romance authors:

Facebook.com/groups/HistRomBookClub

Join the *Rogues to Riches* facebook group for insider info and first looks at future books in the series:

Facebook.com/groups/RoguesToRiches

Check out the *12 Dukes of Christmas* facebook group for giveaways and exclusive content:

Facebook.com/groups/DukesOfChristmas

Check out the *Dukes of War* facebook group for giveaways and exclusive content:

Facebook.com/groups/DukesOfWar

And check out the official website for sneak peeks and more:

www.EricaRidley.com/books

In order, the 12 Dukes of Christmas:

Once Upon a Duke
Kiss of a Duke
Wish Upon a Duke
Never Say Duke
Dukes, Actually
The Duke's Bride
The Duke's Embrace
The Duke's Desire
Dawn With a Duke
One Night With a Duke
Ten Days With a Duke
Forever Your Duke

In order, the Rogues to Riches books are:

Lord of Chance
Lord of Pleasure
Lord of Night
Lord of Temptation
Lord of Secrets
Lord of Vice

In order, the Dukes of War books are:

The Viscount's Tempting Minx (FREE!)
The Earl's Defiant Wallflower
The Captain's Bluestocking Mistress
The Major's Faux Fiancée
The Brigadier's Runaway Bride

The Pirate's Tempting Stowaway
The Duke's Accidental Wife

Want to be the first to know about new releases?

Sign up at http://ridley.vip for members-only exclusives, including advance notice of pre-orders, as well as contests, giveaways, freebies, and 99¢ deals!

ACKNOWLEDGMENTS

As always, I could not have written this book without the invaluable support of my critique partners. Huge thanks go out to Darcy Burke and Eva Devon for their advice and encouragement. You are the best!

My thanks also goes to my editor, Lesley Jones, whose careful eyes catch everything from typos to continuity goofs. Any mistakes are my own.

Lastly, I want to thank the *Rogues to Riches* facebook group, my *Historical Romance Book Club*, and my fabulous street team. Your enthusiasm makes the romance happen.

Thank you so much!

ABOUT THE AUTHOR

Erica Ridley is a *New York Times* and *USA Today* best-selling author of historical romance novels.

In the new *12 Dukes of Christmas* series, enjoy witty, heartwarming Regency romps nestled in a picturesque snow-covered village. After all, nothing heats up a winter night quite like finding oneself in the arms of a duke!

Her two most popular series, the *Dukes of War* and *Rogues to Riches*, feature roguish peers and dashing war heroes who find love amongst the splendor and madness of Regency England.

When not reading or writing romances, Erica can be found riding camels in Africa, zip-lining through rainforests in Central America, or getting hopelessly lost in the middle of Budapest.

~

Let's be friends! Find Erica on:
www.EricaRidley.com